Goddess Girls

ATHENA
THE WISE

READ THE OTHER BOOKS IN THE

GODDESS GIRLS SERIES

ATHENA
THE WISE

JOAN HOLUB & SUZANNE WILLIAMS

Aladdin

NEW YORK   LONDON   TORONTO   SYDNEY

ALADDIN

An imprint of Simon & Schuster Children's Publishing Division

1230 Avenue of the Americas, New York, NY 10020

This Aladdin paperback edition April 2015

Copyright © 2011 by Joan Holub and Suzanne Williams

All rights reserved, including the right of reproduction

in whole or in part in any form.

ALADDIN is a trademark of Simon & Schuster, Inc., and related logo

is a registered trademark of Simon & Schuster, Inc.

For information about special discounts for bulk purchases,

please contact Simon & Schuster Special Sales at 1-866-506-1949

or business@simonandschuster.com.

The Simon & Schuster Speakers Bureau can bring authors to your live event.

For more information or to book an event contact the Simon & Schuster Speakers

Bureau at 1-866-248-3049 or visit our website at www.simonspeakers.com.

Designed by Karin Paprocki

The text of this book was set in Baskerville Handcut Regular.

Manufactured in the United States of America 0415 OFF

2 4 6 8 10 9 7 5 3 1

Library of Congress Control Number 2010938957

ISBN 978-1-4814-5036-2 (pbk)

ISBN 978-1-4424-2098-4 (eBook)

For Sabina Hanson,

who is smart like Athena and as curious as Pandora

–S. W.

For Madison and Skylar Stekly

–J. H.

CONTENTS

1

The New Mortal

WHO'S THAT?" ATHENA ASKED, GESTURING toward an unfamiliar boy as she plunked her tray onto the table where she and her goddessgirl friends always sat for lunch. The entire cafeteria at Mount Olympus Academy was buzzing with excitement over him. Usually she didn't pay much attention to boys, but even *she* couldn't help noticing this one. Dressed in a lion-skin cape—its jaws fit his head like a helmet—

he was tall with dark, curly hair, and bursting with

muscles like Atlas, the school's champion weightlifter.

Aphrodite arched a perfectly shaped eyebrow.

"You haven't heard? His name's Heracles. He was

admitted to the Academy only this morning." A look

of disapproval came into her lovely blue eyes as she

glanced at him. "I'll admit he's cute, but he has abso-

lutely no sense of fashion."

Athena took a bite of her hero sandwich. A lion

cape *was* perhaps overkill as a fashion statement.

"I heard he's a skilled archer," said Artemis. "But

I'll believe it when I see it."

She frowned in his direction. "Word is that he's

mortal, just like Orion. So maybe he's a liar, too."

Orion had been her disappointing first crush, too

stuck on himself to notice anyone else's feelings—especially *hers*. Now she tended to look upon all boys with suspicion, particularly those who reminded her of Orion in any way.

Persephone took a sip from her carton of nectar. "So he's mortal and he dresses weird. That doesn't mean he isn't nice." She was sensitive about stuff like that. Probably because *her* crush, Hades, had often been misunderstood just because he came from the Underworld.

A burst of admiring laughter came from the table where Heracles sat, drawing the girls' eyes. He seemed to have wasted no time in making new friends among the godboys. Several of them, including Hades; Artemis's twin brother, Apollo; Ares; and Poseidon were hanging on his every word. Athena couldn't quite hear what Heracles was saying, but whatever it was probably involved weapons, war, sports, or hunting. In her experience, those were the topics that interested godboys most. Sure enough, moments later Heracles passed around his big, knobby club, which the boys oohed and aahed over. Not to be outdone, Poseidon showed off his trident, and Apollo, his bow.

Aphrodite nudged Athena. "So, what's your opinion?"

Thinking she must have missed part of the conversation, Athena asked, "About what?"

"About Heracles."

Aphrodite, Artemis, and Persephone leaned toward her, as if anxious to hear what she had to say. Athena hesitated. She could well remember how nervous she felt when she first came to MOA less than a year ago.

Most of the godboys and goddessgirls here, including her three best friends, had been together for years by then. They were all so beautiful, handsome, gifted, and amazing. If she'd suspected at the time that they were discussing her—sizing her up and making judgments—she would've felt way more nervous.

"Maybe we should try to put ourselves in *his* sandals and wonder what he's thinking of us, instead of the other way around," she suggested. "He's probably wondering if we're all going to like him. Perhaps he's trying to impress those godboys."

Aphrodite blinked. "I never thought of that."

Persephone smiled at Athena in admiration. "That's beyond brainy thinking, even for you."

"Words of wisdom from the goddessgirl of wisdom herself!" added Artemis.

5

"Thanks," Athena told them. The praise was nice, but honestly, although she knew she was brainy, she wasn't so sure she deserved the title of goddessgirl of *wisdom*. If she were truly wise, she wouldn't have made all the mistakes she'd made since she'd been here at MOA—like flooding the Earth with inventions, taking on too many classes and extracurriculars, and turning Medusa's hair into snakes. Besides, words meant nothing without action. So far, she hadn't done anything herself to welcome Heracles. Well, she could change that.

She finished off her hero sandwich, hoping it would make her feel a little more heroic. Then, gathering her courage, she stood up from the table. "I'm going over to say hi to him. You know, welcome him to the Academy." She hesitated a moment. Putting herself forward like that didn't come easy to her—especially with boys. As her friends looked at her in surprise, she hinted, "Anyone want to come with me?"

Before the others could reply, the school intercom crackled to life. There was a tapping sound, as if someone was repeatedly poking at the button. Then Principal Zeus's voice boomed out of the speaker over the cafeteria door, making everyone jump. "IS THIS THING ON?" *Tap tap tap.* "MS. HYDRA?" *Tap tap tap.* "YOU SURE?" After some more crackling, he finally thundered out his message: "CALLING ATHENA! REPORT TO MY OFFICE. PRONTO. ON THE DOUBLE!" A pause. "OH YEAH, AND BY THE WAY, THIS IS PRINCIPAL ZEUS, YOUR DEAR OL' DAD, IN CASE YOU DIDN'T GUESS!"

Every eye in the cafeteria swung her way. Athena

gulped. Zeus was never one to say please, especially if he was *dis*pleased about something. After all, he was King of the Gods and Ruler of the Heavens, so manners were not his first priority.

"Change of plans, everyone. I'll see you later." Leaving her tray on the table, Athena hurried out the door. Even though—or maybe *because*— Principal Zeus was her dad, she worried about pleasing him more than anyone else at MOA did. Her stomach did acrobatic flips as she rushed down the hall to his office. She racked her brain trying to think if she'd done something wrong. She was making straight As, so surely none of the teachers had complained. But her dad wasn't big on friendly fatherly talks or idle chitchat, either. So what could he possibly want?

2

On Trial

ALL NINE OF MS. HYDRA'S HEADS LOOKED up as Athena entered the front office. "Hello, dear," said the orange head as all the others went back to scanning paperwork, adding figures, or whatever else they'd been doing. "Principal Zeus is waiting for you, so go right in."

"Thanks," said Athena. She started toward Zeus's

door, then turned back for a moment. "Ms. Hydra?"

The administrative assistant's green and purple heads swiveled to look at her.

"I was just wondering if—"

"Yes?" interrupted Ms. Hydra's impatient purple head.

"—if you could tell me what kind of mood he's in?" Athena finished.

"Can't say. He's been holed up in his office all morning."

Just then Zeus threw open his door, knocking it from two of its hinges—something that happened quite often, actually. So often, in fact, that not one of Ms. Hydra's heads batted an eye over it. She just rang a little bell on her desk marked "hinges" to summon a custodian to repair it.

Athena stared up at Zeus's massive head with its wild red hair and curly beard as the principal filled the doorway. "Hi, Dad," she said. "You wanted to see me?"

"You bet I do!" he bellowed. "So what are you doing standing around out there jawing with Ms. Hydra?" He moved a few inches to let her inside. He was almost seven feet tall, with bulging muscles, so he towered over her like a giant as she squeezed past him into the room.

Zeus shut the door behind them, and it swung crazily from its one good hinge, creaking. As usual, her dad's office looked like a tornado had swept through it. Files, scrolls, maps, random pieces from an Olympusopoly board game, and empty bottles of Zeus juice were scattered everywhere. Half-dead plants perched atop dented file cabinets, and several chairs with scorch marks on their cushions sat tilted at odd angles, making the path through the office one big crazy maze.

"Sit!" Zeus commanded as he crossed the room to the huge golden throne behind his desk. As he lowered himself into it, Athena dragged a green chair with a scalloped back to the other side of his desk. She had to empty the scrolls and O-racle-o cookie wrappers from it before she could sit, however.

Then she pointed to several huge sheets of papyrus on top of Zeus's desk. They were covered with sketches. "What are those?" she asked, leaning forward to get a closer look at what seemed to be designs for a new building of some sort.

"Plans for a new temple," Zeus said proudly. "The

people of Olympia are going to dedicate it to little ol' me! Naturally it's being built to my specifications, so I've been gathering all the newest architectural ideas," he went on with growing enthusiasm. He pointed to a stack of *Temple Digest* magazines piled up on the corner of his desk. The cover blurbs read:

- CORINTHIAN, IONIC, OR DORIC? WHAT YOUR CHOICE OF COLUMNS SAYS ABOUT YOU

- HOT NEW TRENDS: DECORATE YOUR TEMPLE WITH AWESOME MORTAL DEEDS

- WOW YOUR WORSHIPPERS WITH WALL-TO-WALL MARBLE!

"I tell you this temple is going to blow every other temple in Greece right out of the water!"

"Impressive," said Athena. "And congratulations!" She was surprised at how excited he was. It wasn't like this was the first temple built in his honor. He was the biggest, baddest god of them all, so people on Earth practically fell all over themselves to win his favor.

The flat, golden bracelets that encircled Zeus's wrists flashed as he shoved the drawings and magazines onto the floor so he could prop his sandled feet on the desktop. "But enough chitchat. That's not what I called you here to talk about today."

Warily, Athena sat back in her chair. "Is it about my studies? I've been getting all As, so I don't see how—"

Zeus waved away her concern. "Not at all. Your teachers have told me you're doing brilliantly."

"Oh, good." Athena felt her shoulders relax.

Suddenly a funny look came into Zeus's eyes. He thumped the side of his head with the palm of his meaty hand. Tiny thunderbolts shot out between his fingers, scorching the wall to the right of his desk, and setting his beard on fire. Zeus blew on his chest quickly to put out the flames. "Thanks a lot, Metis," he grumbled, speaking to Athena's mom, who was a fly inside his head. "I wish you could see what you just made me do! Okay, okay," he said after a pause. "Don't get your wings in a twist. I know it's no picnic for you, being cooped up inside my head. Yes, I'm sure she understands, but I'll tell her."

"Tell me what?" Athena asked. Having a fly as a mother was just plain weird. Plus she couldn't even *see* her mom. Sometimes she wondered what it would be like to have a *real* mother, one who—besides looking a lot like her—could cook and sew and comfort her with hugs. Or at least talk to her!

Zeus glanced at her. "Your mother says she's sorry she can't play a more active role in your life. She hopes you know she loves you just the same."

Athena gulped. Had Metis read her mind some-how? "Yes, I know," she said guiltily.

"Good," said Zeus. "Now kindly buzz off."

Startled, Athena rose from her chair.

"Not you!" Zeus said hastily. "I was speaking to your mother again."

"Oh!" Athena sat back down.

Zeus's big feet thumped to the floor, making everything in the room jump. He clasped his big hands together on top of his desk and leaned forward. "You must be wondering why I asked you here."

"Well, yes, actually," she admitted.

Her dad's eyes strayed to the drawings he'd knocked aside for a moment, then his gaze returned to her. "I've invited a new boy to MOA," he began.

"You mean Heracles?" interrupted Athena. What

could the new boy possibly have to do with her?

Zeus nodded. "That's the one." He paused. "The thing is, he's here on trial."

"On trial?" Athena repeated. What was that supposed to mean? And why was he telling *her*?

"I'm giving the boy a week to prove himself," Zeus said. "To find out if he truly belongs here."

"I see," said Athena, but she didn't. Why require this of Heracles when MOA's previous new mortal student, Orion, had been admitted without trial? On the other hand, Orion *had* caused a lot of trouble at MOA, so maybe that's why Zeus decided to change the rules.

"Heracles has more brawn than brains," Zeus confided bluntly. "And he's hotheaded. At times he goes off like an out-of-control chariot that's about to lose a wheel."

"Really?" Athena said. "You know that for sure?" Maybe her friends weren't the only ones quick to judge the new boy.

Zeus nodded grimly. "I have a report from his former school. Seems he and the music teacher had a run-in. Sour notes were exchanged. The long and short of it is that Heracles wound up smashing a lyre over the teacher's head."

"Godness!" Athena exclaimed. She wondered why he was he telling her this. Did he want to warn her away from Heracles? If the boy was a problem at his other school, why had Zeus even invited him here? If she, like everyone else at school, weren't just a little bit scared of her dad, she'd ask.

"Here's why I'm telling you all this," Zeus said, as if he, too, could read her mind. "I want you to keep an eye on Heracles for me. Befriend him. Offer him some guidance."

Athena's gray eyes widened. "What? Why me?" This wasn't at all what she'd expected him to say.

Zeus grinned at her, practically blinding her with his white teeth. "Who better than my favorite daughter in the whole wide universe? Besides, you *are* the goddessgirl of wisdom, right?"

Ye gods. It was the second time in an hour that someone had reminded her of that! "Well, yeah," she said uncertainly. Half of her was worried that she'd fail to live up to the title, but the other half felt flattered that Zeus had chosen her—that he thought she could help Heracles. She guessed he must not think there was any danger of a lyre getting smashed over *her* head.

"Come on, Theeny," Zeus wheedled. "Pretty please with nectar on top?"

Athena smiled. How could she resist when he asked so nicely? And she did want to please him. "Okay," she said. "I'll do it."

"Excellent!" boomed Zeus. Jumping up from his throne, he reached over the desk, scooped her out of her chair, and gathered her up in a big bear hug.

"Oompf," said Athena, struggling to breathe. Electricity fizzled from his fingertips, zapping her.

Finally he released her and plopped back down onto his throne. As Athena sat catching her breath, he reached for the temple designs and began to study them once more. "Um . . . are we done here?" she asked after a minute.

Zeus glanced up, looking surprised to see that

she was still there. "Oh, hi, Theeny. Did you want something?"

"Um, no, I'll just be going, I guess." Standing, she began sidling out of the room. As she stepped over a stack of files, she accidentally flattened an empty can of Zapple. *Crack!* The sound must've drawn Zeus's attention because when she was almost at the door, his head popped up over one of the file cabinets behind her.

"One more thing," he said, as she pushed the broken door aside.

She looked over her shoulder at him. "Yes, sir?"

"Don't tell him I asked you to help him."

Her brows rose. "But—"

"Oh, and one more thing," he interrupted.

"Yes?" she asked again.

His piercing blue eyes bored into her gray ones as he gave her his King of the Gods, Ruler of the Heavens–look. "Don't let me down," he commanded.

"Okay," she said, because really, what else could she say? Then she skedaddled before he could come up with one *more* thing.

3

Revenge‑ology

WHAT HAVE I GOTTEN MYSELF INTO NOW?
Athena wondered as she left Zeus's office. She started
down the gleaming marble-tiled main hall, so busy
thinking that she hardly noticed the beautiful golden
fountains and murals illustrating the glorious deeds
of gods and goddesses as she passed by them.

She and Heracles hadn't even spoken to each other, yet her dad expected them to become best buds? And Zeus had made it clear he'd be very disappointed if she didn't succeed at—at what, exactly? Some goddessgirl of wisdom *she* was. She'd agreed to help Heracles without really knowing what Zeus expected her to do. Zeus said Heracles was hotheaded. Was she supposed to keep him out of trouble, then? Or maybe tutor him in his worst subjects? Oh, why hadn't she asked more questions when she had the chance?

Veering left, she dodged past a godboy, with curved horns and a scaly tail, and two goddessgirls, with pink hair and large wings, to stop at her locker. "Number one eighty three, open for me," she chanted. Her locker door swung open, and she grabbed the textscroll for her next class from the neat stack inside. A lyrebell sounded just as her locker door swung shut again.

Athena glanced up at the herald who stood on the balcony at the end of the hall. "Class will begin in two minutes," he announced in a loud, important voice. Then he struck his lyrebell again with a little hammer. *Ping! Ping! Ping!*

Athena waved at him. He was rather pompous and took pride in always keeping a straight face, so all the students had made a game of trying to startle him. It didn't work this time. Turning, she hurried off to Revenge-ology. Her teacher, Ms. Nemesis, stood just inside the door, nodding a curt greeting as each student entered the classroom. She was glad she was on time because Ms. Nemesis was big on punishments and just desserts—and that didn't mean the sweet kind. Still, Athena secretly admired her because she was bold and independent. A strong woman, just like Athena wanted to be.

Skirting her teacher's large wings, Athena walked toward her seat. As she passed Medusa, her snaky hair writhed and hissed. Athena leaned away.

Medusa shrugged. "Sorry, my reptiles just don't like flybabies. What can I do?"

Gorgonhead, thought Athena, but she didn't say it because she wasn't mean like *some* people. It was no secret that Athena's mom was a fly, but Medusa—and her two sisters—were the only ones mean enough to tease her about it. Ignoring her, Athena continued on past. After taking her seat, she set her textscroll on top of her desk, then reached into her bag for a feather pen.

Bam! The loud thump made Athena jump.

"Hey, watch it with that thing!" growled Medusa.

Athena glanced up to see Heracles just a few seats ahead of her, struggling to balance a stack of textscrolls. His club lay on the floor next to Medusa's desk, where it had fallen.

"Sorry," he said to Medusa. As he stooped to pick up his club, her snakes flicked out their tongues and darted toward him. Quicker than Zeus could shoot a lightning bolt, Heracles grabbed a handful of the snakes in his free hand and began to squeeze.

"Stop!" screamed Medusa. "You're strangling them!"

From the front of the room Ms. Nemesis shot Heracles a stern look. "Is there a problem?"

Sheepishly, Heracles let go of the snakes. They drooped, seeming dazed but unharmed. Ms. Nemesis pointed him toward an empty seat across the aisle from Athena. "Sit, please."

"'Kay." Ambling casually to the desk, he tossed his textscrolls on top of it, and then slung his club onto the floor beside his chair. *Wham!* As he sat, Medusa turned her head to glare at him.

Athena leaned toward him. "Don't look her in the eye," she whispered quickly. "She turns mortals to stone."

Heracles' hands flew up to shield his eyes. "Thanks for the warning," he said, peeking at Athena between his fingers.

"No problem," she said. Maybe guiding Heracles wasn't going to be so difficult after all. He'd already acted on her first piece of advice. What luck that he was enrolled in one of her classes!

Athena glanced toward the front of the room. Ms. Nemesis was writing something on the board, her back to the class. At the nape of her neck, a shiny gold clip in the shape of a sword held back her golden hair. Athena had often thought that if Aphrodite had had a mother, she might have looked something like Ms. Nemesis. Only Ms. Nemesis was a great deal graver and more serious than Aphrodite. And grouchy. And winged.

Turning toward the class, Ms. Nemesis pointed to the question she'd written on the board. "What is vengeance?" she read aloud.

Lots of hands shot up in the air, including Athena's. Ms. Nemesis called on Medusa.

"If someone does something monstrous or diabolical or just plain rotten to you"—Medusa broke off, narrowing her eyes at Heracles, who ducked to avoid her gaze—"or your snakes," she added, "then you get to do something bad back to them."

"Okay," said Ms. Nemesis. "Can anyone expand on or improve Medusa's answer?"

The mortals in class who had raised their hands earlier withdrew them as Medusa's eyes swept the room. Athena kept her hand in the air.

"Yes?" said Ms. Nemesis.

"The thing is," Athena said, "Vengeance is really revenge. And for revenge to be fair, there needs to be balance." She hesitated.

Ms. Nemesis nodded. "Keep going."

"Well," said Athena, toying with her blue feather pen. "It's the 'eye for an eye, tooth for a tooth' idea. The punishment for a wrong should fit the deed. For example, if someone kicks you, you *could* kick them back, but cutting off their leg would be going too far."

drop his club instead. It landed on his foot.

"Ow! Ow! Ow!" he yelled. Clasping his foot in both hands, he hopped up and down on one leg.

Students gaped at him in surprise. "Serves him right," Medusa muttered with a smirk.

Ms. Nemesis hurried over. "Are you okay?"

As if he'd just noticed that everyone was staring at him, Heracles' face turned as red as a pomegranate. "I'm fine," he mumbled. "At least I will be when my foot stops throbbing."

"You're sure?" asked Ms. Nemesis.

Heracles felt his foot carefully. "Nothing broken," he said. "Except my pride."

Several students chuckled, but seeing he was all right, they began to leave.

Athena knelt to help Heracles pick up his

textscrolls, pleased that he'd had a sense of humor about the mishap. "You might want to stow some of these in your locker," she suggested. "And maybe you don't need to carry around your club all the time either."

"Good idea about the scrolls," said Heracles. "But my club stays with me." They walked out of the room together. "You know," he told her, "that was kind of embarrassing back there. And on my first day of school."

Athena laughed. "On *my* first day here, a toy horse I'd had since I was a toddler rolled out of my bag in the middle of class."

"Whoa," said Heracles. He grinned. "I guess I shouldn't feel *too* sorry for myself, then." He motioned with the tip of his club toward a wall of lockers. "I think

I'll take your advice before my next class. See you."

"Wait," Athena said impulsively. "I'm meeting up with some friends after school at the Supernatural Market. Want to come? They make the best ambrosia shakes ever."

"Sounds like fun." He leaned his club up against a locker, then twirled the lock on his. "Where is the Supernatural Market?"

"On the other side of the sports fields, beyond the gymnasium," she said. "How about if I meet you by the stairs up to the dorms at the end of the day? We can walk together."

"Great!" said Heracles. "Catch you later, then."

Athena waved to him as she started off to her next class. Maybe Zeus had judged Heracles too harshly. Yes, he could use some guidance—the kind that all new students needed. While it was true that he'd almost strangled some of Medusa's snakes, probably everyone at MOA had wanted to do that at one time or another. And he *had* managed to cool down before he did any real harm. Perhaps he'd been *provoked* into beaning his music teacher with the lyre as well! Anyway, she liked his sense of humor. She smiled to herself. It didn't matter if Zeus was right or wrong about Heracles. Now that she was getting to know him, she was happy to have an excuse to keep an eye on him!

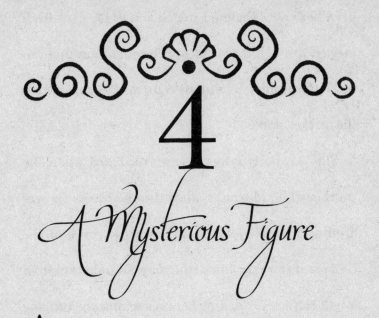

4

A Mysterious Figure

ATHENA TAPPED HER FOOT IMPATIENTLY.
She'd been waiting by the marble staircase for
nearly half hour. Where in the world was Heracles?
The hallway was empty. Her friends would be at the
Supernatural Market by now. They were probably
wondering where she was. If Heracles had changed
his mind about coming, it would've been nice of him

to let her know. Feeling irritated and let down, Athena pushed through the Academy's bronze doors and ran down the granite steps to the courtyard to start toward the market alone.

She was halfway across the courtyard when she overheard loud voices and glimpsed two figures arguing at the edge of the olive grove that grew on the courtyard's far side. One of the voices sounded familiar. Was it Heracles'? Shading her eyes against the sun, she squinted at the figures. They were both boys. She didn't recognize the one on the left, but the one on the right was wearing a lion pelt. Definitely Heracles!

Feeling confused, Athena tried to think about what to do. She felt certain Aphrodite would have advised her to ignore him and keep walking, to punish him for standing her up. But *she* wanted an explanation! Should she interrupt him and ask for one? As she stood there, undecided, Heracles broke away from the other figure, who melted into the grove.

"Athena!" he called out. Holding his club against his shoulder, he jogged over to where she stood. "Sorry I'm late," he said. "Are you mad?"

"A little," she admitted. Then she grinned. "But I'll get over it. Do you still want to go?"

"Yup!"

They started toward the sports fields at the edge of campus. Athena had to walk fast to keep up with Heracles' long strides. "Who was that boy you were talking to?" she asked after a minute.

Heracles frowned. "My cousin. Eurystheus."

"Sounds like you weren't happy to see him," Athena said, huffing and puffing a little.

"You got that right," Heracles muttered.

Athena raised an eyebrow. "Something the matter?"

Heracles shook his head. "It's nothing. Nothing I can't take care of, anyway."

She'd promised not to tell Heracles that Zeus had asked her to help, but that didn't mean she couldn't *offer.* Still, boys could be so touchy about anyone thinking them weak in any way. Especially one who seemed to rely so much on his brawny strength. So Athena said carefully, "If you ever find yourself in trouble here or need help, will you ask me?"

He looked at her in surprise, then shrugged. "I guess so." Moments later, he pointed to a huge, round building to the left of the grassy field they were crossing just then. "Is that the gymnasium?"

"Uh-huh," said Athena. "Sometimes the school

holds dances there, and Apollo's band plays. It's open to the sky in the center."

"Wow," said Heracles. "My old school's gymnasium wasn't even half as big. It sure was nice of Principal Zeus to invite me here." He hesitated. "Guess he's your dad, huh?"

"Yes." The intercom announcement during lunch had certainly made that clear! Athena wondered if Heracles also knew that her mom was a fly. If so, at least he was tactful enough not to mention it.

When they arrived at the doors to the market, Artemis's three hounds, who weren't allowed inside, barked joyfully and bounded up to them, their tails wagging. Amby, the beagle, wiggled all over as Athena reached down to pet him, while Nectar and Suez growled, seeming wary of Heracles' lion-skin cape. He held out a hand for the dogs to sniff. Within moments they were licking his fingers and yipping playfully, as if they'd always been friends.

Athena gave Amby one last pat on the head. "See you later, boys," she said, leaving them behind as she and Heracles entered the market.

They walked past shelves of snacks and a rack filled with copies of the latest issue of *Teen Scrollazine*. Noticing that Orion was on the cover wearing a big bright smile, Athena flipped the magazine around, hoping Artemis hadn't seen it on her way into the market. "It's a long story," she told Heracles, when he looked at her curiously. Then they went on to a big round table at the back of the store where Athena's friends sat drinking their shakes. Her roommate, Pandora, and Pheme, the goddessgirl of rumor, were there too. Aphrodite waved her over. "About time you got here!"

"Heracles!" shouted Apollo. "What are you doing here?"

"*I* was invited," Heracles replied with a grin. "And you?"

Apollo laughed. "Touché." He motioned to an empty chair between him and Poseidon, and Heracles sat.

At the far end of the table, Persephone pulled Hades up by the hand. "We'll go get more shakes."

Artemis got up too. "I'll help."

"Interesting," murmured Aphrodite as Athena took the chair between Pheme and her. "Guess you managed to introduce yourself to Heracles after all."

"Don't go getting any of your romantic ideas," Athena said, keeping her voice low so that Pheme wouldn't hear. "I was just being friendly when I asked him here."

Aphrodite smiled. "That's what they all say."

Pheme leaned toward them. Her eyes gleamed as she licked her orange-glossed lips. "Did I miss something?" Her words puffed above her head in little cloud letters that vanished soon after they were spoken.

"Nothing important," Athena said quickly.

"Oh." Scraping a spoon along the bottom of her empty shake glass, Pheme sighed with disappointment.

To cheer her up, and because it was true, Athena said, "That's a really cute chiton you're wearing." Dark green looked good on Pheme, complementing her fair complexion and spiky orange hair. And Athena could see that the quality of the woven fabric was exceptionally good.

Pheme brightened at the compliment. "Thanks. I got it from Arachne."

"Arachne's Sewing Supplies?" asked Athena. "In the Immortal Marketplace? I thought they just sold yarns, thread, and fabrics."

Pheme shook her head. "I didn't buy this chiton at the mall. I bought it from Arachne herself."

"Arachne is a real person?" said Athena. "I thought that was just the name of the shop."

Pheme stared at her, wide-eyed. "The shop is named in her honor. Seriously, though, you've never heard of her?"

"Isn't she that mortal girl who's supposed to be such a terrific weaver?" asked Aphrodite. "I hear she's quite famous down on Earth. I forget where she's from, though."

"Hypaepa," said Pheme. "It's this tiny little town at the foot of Mount Aepos."

Athena felt embarrassed that she hadn't known about the girl. After all, Athena had *invented* weaving. "I wonder why I've never heard of her," she said aloud.

Aphrodite laughed. "Maybe because you spend too much time with your nose stuck in your textscrolls?"

"You should pay more attention to what's going on around you," said Pheme. "You'd be surprised how many interesting things you can learn."

Athena smiled. It was just the kind of advice you'd expect from the goddessgirl of rumor. Pheme had a point, though. Athena *should* pay a little more attention to things going on down on Earth. And she couldn't help feeling flattered that mortal girls were taking an interest in weaving, a craft she had invented. Perhaps she should champion their successes. She made a mental note to visit this Arachne sometime soon.

Persephone, Hades, and Artemis were back with another half-dozen ambrosia shakes. "Thanks," said Athena as Persephone handed her one. She also gave one to Heracles.

"Mmm," he said, a few moments later. He glanced at the shakes that Hades and Artemis still held. "You can just leave all of those with me."

Everyone laughed. "Is that lion skin for real?" Pandora asked, staring at Heracles from across the table.

"Sure," said Heracles. "Is your blue hair for real?"

Pandora blushed, reaching up to pat her hair, which was streaked with blue and gold. "It's the school colors, didn't you know?"

Athena hid a smile. For as long as she'd known her, Pandora's hair had looked like that. As a sign of her curiosity, her bangs were plastered against her forehead in the shape of a question mark. But sometimes Pandora's curiosity bordered on rudeness. Heracles had just given her a taste of her own medicine.

Now Apollo nudged Heracles with his elbow. "Tell the girls that story you told us at lunch."

"Yeah, the one about how you got your lion cape," prompted Poseidon.

Heracles shrugged. "They don't want to hear about that."

"I do," said Artemis, "as long as you stick to the facts." Orion, her disastrous crush, had often exaggerated his abilities in the stories he told. Heracles glanced around the table at the other goddessgirls. They nodded.

"Go on, tell us," said Athena. It was a story she really wanted to hear.

"Okay, but I hope you aren't squeamish," said Heracles, looking a little worried. "Truth is that I had to kill this lion because it was a big problem for the people of Nemea. Afterward I skinned it, and now I wear its pelt." He smiled at Artemis. "And those are the facts."

Poseidon thumped his trident on the floor. "You left out all the good stuff. Tell them about the lion's impenetrable skin!"

"Impene-what?" asked Persephone.

"Heracles' arrows weren't any good against the lion," Hades explained. "Its skin was so thick and tough, the arrows just bounced off."

Picking up the story, Apollo began miming the

actions as he described them. "So he chased the lion into its lair, wrestled it to the ground, and snapped its neck with his bare hands."

"Godness!" Aphrodite exclaimed. "How gruesome! I can't help feeling sorry for the lion."

"Don't," said Poseidon, shaking his head. "That lion was a menace. It got its kicks out of terrorizing the Nemean people, killing their farm animals, and—" He paused as if unsure whether to go on.

"And *worse*," Heracles finished.

Athena wasn't sure what *worse* meant, but she thought it was nice of Heracles to want to spare them the grisly details. Still, there was one thing that mystified her. "If the lion's hide was impenetrable, how did you manage to skin it?"

Heracles ran his hand down the side of his pelt. "I

puzzled over that for the longest time," he admitted. "It could have come back to life if I hadn't, so I had to find a way. Can you guess?"

Athena thought for a moment. Then in a flash, the answer came to her. She snapped her fingers. "The claws!" she exclaimed. "You cut the pelt with the lion's own claws."

"Wow," said Heracles. He looked at her admiringly. "You sure figured that out fast. It would have saved me some time if you'd been with me."

The other godboys laughed, but Athena felt sure Heracles had meant his comment to be serious, not funny.

"Why couldn't the Nemeans kill the lion themselves?" asked Pandora. "Why did *you* have to kill it for them?"

"Um, well," said Heracles, looking a little secretive. "I just did." Then he abruptly changed the subject, asking Apollo and Artemis about a new archery competition they were practicing for.

Was Heracles hiding something? Athena wondered. *His answer to Pandora's question had been pretty vague. And then there was his cousin turning up so unexpectedly. Heracles hadn't seemed to want to talk about that, either. Hmm. Maybe, just maybe, Zeus was right to be concerned about him.*

When it was almost time for dinner, everyone started back to the Academy. The godboys clowned around, mimicking some of their teachers and throwing fake punches, as they walked ahead of the goddessgirls. Athena kept an eye on Heracles as the girls chatted among themselves. As they crossed the courtyard, he broke away from the other boys.

Athena watched him head for the trail that led down to Earth. She followed her friends into MOA's main hall, but when they began to climb the stairs to the dorms, she called out, "I'll catch you later, okay?"

Artemis, Aphrodite, and Persephone paused a few steps above her. "Please don't tell us you're going to go study at the library again," said Artemis. "It's Friday night, for godness sake."

Athena laughed. "Okay, I won't tell you that. And anyway, that's not it. There's just something I need to do." Dashing outside before they could question her, she headed for the trail Heracles had taken. Once she reached it, ash, olive, and date palm trees as well as clusters of grapevines, ivy, and hyacinth shielded her from view.

Quickly she concentrated on bringing into her mind an image of her favorite bird. As she held on to that image, her body became smaller and lighter, and she began to sprout feathers. Her arms became wings, and her eyes grew rounder and wider until she had shape-shifted into a big brown owl! With a carefree *hoot*, she flapped her wings and rose into the air.

5

Too Many Heads

FLYING OVER THE TRAIL, ATHENA SOON

spotted Heracles dressed in his lion skin and swing-

ing his club. She followed him through forests and

valleys, past several small towns to a place called

Lerna. According to rumor—no doubt Pheme was the

source—a Hydra who was a distant cousin of Zeus's

administrative assistant lived here. Only *this* Hydra

was the black sheep of the Hydra family. Like Ms. Hydra at school, it was a serpent with nine heads, but unlike her, it ravaged fields and devoured livestock, creating no end of trouble for the poor people who lived in this area.

Heracles skirted the edge of town and scaled a small cliff, to arrive at the edge of a desolate swamp that was bordered by a few straggly, fire-blackened trees. With his club raised high, he approached a cave in the cliff.

Athena flew down to perch in a tree a short distance away.

"Come on out, Nineheads!" Heracles shouted. "I know you're in there!"

Moments later all nine of the dreadful Hydra's heads popped out of the cave door that was the

56

entrance to its lair. "Just who do you think you are, disturbing me here?" it roared, fire shooting out of its mouths.

Heracles wrinkled his nose. "P.U.! That's some bad breath you've got. Is that how you kill your prey? You just knock 'em dead?"

"Very funny," said the Hydra. Its wings fanned the air as it advanced toward Heracles on scaly legs that ended in long, pointy claws.

Heracles held his club out in front of him as if it were a shield. "Don't come any closer!" he yelled.

The Hydra just cackled. "You think that knobby wooden stick's gonna save you? Go ahead, big guy. I dare you to try to knock off one of my heads. Just see what happens!"

"All right, then, I will!" Heracles brought his club

up to his shoulder. His arm muscles rippled as he swung it hard at the Hydra's closest head. *Thwack!*

Ye gods! Athena's owl eyes blinked in dismay as the Hydra's head flew through the air. It landed on the ground near her tree and rolled down the hill. But when she glanced back up at the Hydra, she saw that two more heads had popped up to replace the head that Heracles had knocked off. Now it was technically more of a *Tenheads*.

"Ha-ha!" chortled the Hydra. "You'll have to do better than that. Come on, big guy, do your worst!"

Heracles swung again. This time he managed to knock off two heads, but immediately four *more* heads sprouted up.

Make that a Twelveheads, thought Athena. This was turning into a math lesson.

The Hydra laughed. "Ho-ho-ho! Surprised you, didn't I?" It whipped its tail around, almost sweeping Heracles off his feet with it. But at the last moment he dodged out of the way, and the Hydra's tail slammed the ground. "Oops, missed!"

Red with fury, Heracles swung his club again and again, but only succeeded in multiplying the Hydra's heads.

As much as Athena admired Heracles' courage and strength, she couldn't help fearing for his life. He was mortal after all. He could die! Couldn't he see that this strategy wasn't working?

"Okay, you . . . you buttheads!" blustered Heracles.

"Ignoramus! You've got about as much smarts as that club of yours!" taunted the Hydra as its heads continued to sprout.

Heracles tried to hide it, but he looked a little hurt and embarrassed. *Had he been teased like this before?* Athena wondered. Still, right at that moment, she was inclined to agree with the Hydra. Heracles was so busy taking action that he wasn't thinking straight.

Just then the Hydra's tail lashed out again. Heracles jumped back, but not far enough. The tail coiled around his ankles. In an instant, he was whisked into the air. Held upside down, he dangled in front of the Hydra's many dragonlike heads. Its mouths opened wide to reveal dozens and dozens of dagger-sharp teeth.

Alarmed into action, Athena dropped down from the tree. Shedding her owl disguise for her goddess form, she settled at the Hydra's feet. "Hey!" she shouted. "Let my friend go!"

Still hanging upside down, Heracles twisted around to peer at her. "Where did you come from?"

The Hydra's many heads looked from Heracles to Athena. "Lovely," they chorused, smacking their many lips. "A main course *and* dessert!"

"I've always heard that two heads are better than one," Athena called out quickly. "But you must have, what, thirty now?"

The Hydra peered down at her, a look of confusion in its many eyes.

"Don't tell me you don't know how many heads you have?" Athena said in pretend amazement.

"Well, of course we know," said the middle head. "Just a sec. I'll count. One, two, three . . ." It got up to twelve, and then faltered.

Another head took over. "Wait a second, I think you

skipped one." It started over again. "One, two, three, four . . ."

Heracles, though upside-down, still had his club. Thinking quick, he swung it in a high arc and knocked off three heads.

"Stop that!" the Hydra's middle head scolded as six heads popped up to take their places. "You're messing up our count."

"Set me down, then," Heracles demanded.

"Oh, all right," the Hydra said grumpily.

Heracles winked at Athena as the Hydra lowered him to the ground. "Don't forget to count the head that's counting," he said as soon as he was upright again.

"Huh?" said the head that was currently going at it.

"Oh, let me do the head count," groused yet another

head, possibly number thirty-two. "You're lousy at math."

"You're not much better," groused head number eighteen.

"Am too."

"Are not."

As the heads began to argue, Athena moved closer to the Hydra. She motioned for Heracles to do the same. The monster automatically stepped backward toward the narrow entrance to its lair. It didn't seem to notice that, gradually, Athena and Heracles were herding it back inside.

"If anyone should do the counting, it's me," said a head on the far left. "I'm the one with a head for numbers!"

"Ha!" said the head beside him. "Two days ago you

told me that five is four plus one, but then yesterday you said that five is three plus two! You can't even get your story straight!"

The left head rolled its eyes. "Oh, yeah? Well, you said it's seven minus two, and I happen to know it's ten divided by two. What's that about?"

Heracles and Athena grinned at each other. "I think we're finally making some headway in all this," Athena joked as they slowly but surely corralled the Hydra. Fitting its countless heads through the narrow cave entrance in the cliff was a tight squeeze, but finally, it was completely inside its lair again!

By now all of the heads were either trying to count, or arguing about who was best at math. Some began to head-butt others so forcefully that more heads popped off, only to be replaced by still more. Soon there was hardly any headroom in the lair at all. Though it hadn't realized it yet, the Hydra was trapped!

"Success!" cheered Heracles, punching his fist in the air.

Athena grinned. "So what do you think? Should we *head* back to school now?"

Heracles returned her grin. "Yup." He pointed the tip of his club toward the Hydra. "I guess *you* won't be bothering the people of Lerna again!" he called.

"Huh?" chorused a hundred or more heads. When the Hydra realized the two of them were getting away, it lunged toward the cave's entrance, trying to get out. But with so many heads now, it couldn't fit through the narrow opening, no matter how closely the heads rearranged themselves. Athena and Heracles could still hear the Hydra head-banging and arguing with itself after they'd climbed up the cliff and started toward MOA.

"You were great back there," Heracles told her admiringly. "Thanks for your help."

Score! thought Athena. She'd done what Zeus had asked, and Heracles had actually thanked her. She was pleased with herself for showing him that violence wasn't the only way to solve a problem.

Heracles took a rolled-up sheet of papyrus from his pelt and unrolled it.

Athena could see that the sheet had something written on it. "What's that?" she asked.

"My to-do list," he told her. Frowning slightly, he ran his finger down it. "Two down, ten to go."

Under her breath, Athena said a little spell, whipping up a breeze. The papyrus sheet went flying, and she caught it. "Hmm," she said, glancing at it. "#1 Kill lion. #2 Fight Hydra. #3 Capture—"

"Give that back!" yelled Heracles. He lunged toward her, trying to grab the list, but she sidestepped him and whipped it behind her.

"What'll you do if I keep it?" she teased. "Knock off *my* head?" He looked so frustrated, though, that she took pity on him and handed the list back. Scowling, Heracles rolled it up tightly and stuck it back in his pelt.

They walked on in silence for a few minutes. It was evening by now. Their shadows lengthened as they started through a meadow filled with lovely wildflowers whose names Athena didn't know, but which Persephone could have ticked off without a pause. Finally she said, "Sorry I teased you. But can't you tell me what's going on?"

67

"No," said Heracles.

Athena shot him a glance. "No, you can't? Or no, you won't?"

"Both." Then almost to himself, he said, "Well, I guess he never *said* I couldn't tell anyone."

"Who's *he*?" she asked. "Your cousin? Does he have some kind of hold over you? Or is that list just an elaborate dare?"

"No," said Heracles, shaking his head. "Cousin Eurystheus gets to come up with the tasks, but it was the oracle that told me what I needed to do."

Athena wrinkled her brow in confusion. "Needed to do?" she echoed. "For what reason? I don't get it."

Heracles sighed. "Look, MOA is a much better school than the one I went to on earth. I mean, my school was ba-ad. To give you an idea, I was the smartest kid in it. Obviously I wanted to switch schools, so I consulted an oracle at one of your dad's temples." He paused. "She told me that I could earn a permanent place at the Academy—and even a chance at future immortality—if I completed twelve tasks she called "labors."

"I didn't think that sounded so hard until I found out Eurystheus would get to decide what the labors would be." He frowned. "That weaselly runt has had it in for me ever since we were kids. He hates me because even though I'm younger than him, I've always been bigger and stronger."

"Hmm," said Athena. Suddenly suspicious, she asked, "Does Principal Zeus know about these twelve labors?"

"Dunno," said Heracles. "Maybe. Maybe not. All

I know is that the first part of the oracle's prediction came true. I got a letter from your dad inviting me to the Academy. You can't imagine how excited I was!"

Athena smiled. "Yes, I can." After all, the very same thing had happened to her.

"The thing is the oracle said I'd only have until the end of the school day on Friday to complete the labors. If I don't, she predicted I'll lose my chance at immortality *and* be kicked out of the Academy."

"I see," said Athena, her mind spinning. It was a secret among the gods that oracles were mere portals through which the gods spoke to mortals. And the oracle in question belonged to one of *Zeus's* temples. So that meant the labors had to be Zeus's idea! But he probably hadn't realized at first that Heracles' cousin was going to make them. Now that her dad did know, it was no surprise he'd asked her to keep an eye on Heracles. Pleaded with her to do it, actually. Practically *warned* her not to let him down! He probably felt a little guilty. And poor Heracles had no idea the whole thing was Zeus's idea.

Athena opened her mouth to speak and then closed it again. She was dying to tell Heracles that Principal Zeus was on his side, but she couldn't, of course, without admitting that her dad thought Heracles needed help to succeed. He seemed like the kind of boy who'd be embarrassed by that. "Let me think," she said instead. "Today's Friday. So that gives you what? Seven days to complete ten more tasks?"

"Exactly," said Heracles.

"Why, that's less than one day per task!" Athena exclaimed worriedly. "What's next on your list?"

Heracles glanced away from her. "I don't want to tell you," he said. "You're her friend, and you probably won't like it."

Athena's heart leaped into her throat. What could he mean by that?

6

Third Labor

W HEN THEY BROKE THROUGH THE CLOUDS
at the top of Mount Olympus, the Academy loomed
before them. It was a majestic sight—one that Athena
never tired of. Five stories high and built of polished
white stone, MOA was surrounded on all sides by
dozens of Ionic columns. Sculpted below its peaked
rooftop were expertly chiseled low-relief friezes

depicting famous scholarly feats of the gods and goddesses.

"Awesome, isn't it?" said Heracles.

Athena nodded. "Yes, it is." Soon they'd be going inside and she'd lose her chance to find out about his next labor. She decided to try again. "You've got to tell me what your next task is! I promise I won't get mad, no matter what it is."

Heracles hesitated for several long seconds, but at last he gave in. "Oh, all right. I have to capture one of Artemis's deer and show it to Eurystheus."

"Ye gods!" Athena exclaimed. Like her three dogs, the white deer were special to Artemis. She'd had them as pets ever since second grade. Zeus allowed the four golden-horned deer to stay on the school grounds, and sometimes they pulled Artemis's chariot.

Athena thought carefully. "You only have to capture *one* deer, right?"

Heracles nodded.

"And you could do that without harming it, then return it right after Eurystheus has seen it?"

Heracles' face lit up. "That's a brilliant idea!" Athena wasn't sure she wanted to know which part he thought was brilliant—the returning it part or the not harming it part. He seemed a little too fond of his club for her liking.

"Okay," said Athena. "I think we can nail that one. So what's labor number four?"

"We?" Heracles said, eyeing her.

She nodded. "The deer know me. It'll save time if you let me help."

"Makes sense." Heracles reached under his pelt

and took out his scroll list. Quickly he unrolled and scanned it. "Capture the Erymanthian boar," he read aloud.

Athena sighed. "Your cousin isn't very imaginative, is he? All these tasks seem to have the same pattern. *Boar*-ing!"

Heracles shrugged. "You don't get to pick your relatives."

"True," said Athena. A disloyal thought about her mother the fly flitted through her head. Dismissing it, she said, "First things first. The deer are usually grazing on the lawn behind the Academy this time of day. We'll ask Artemis's permission to borrow one of them." If she lets us, we might have just enough time to show the deer to Eurystheus before nightfall.

Raising an eyebrow, Heracles asked, "Do you think she'll agree?"

"I'll convince her," said Athena, trying to sound more confident than she actually was. After all, Artemis might just say no.

They'd reached the granite steps that led up to the bronze doors of the Academy. "Wait here," Athena told him. "I'll run upstairs and see if Artemis is in her room." Because of her problems with Orion, Artemis was still suspicious of Heracles. Athena figured she had a better chance at getting permission to borrow a deer if she asked alone.

"Good idea," Heracles agreed. "Ms. Hydra told me boys aren't allowed on the girls' floor." As he sat down on one of the steps to wait, Athena dashed up the steps, through the front doors, and up the marble staircase to the girls' dorm on the fourth floor. But when she knocked on Artemis's door there was no answer. No dogs barked, either, so she was obviously out. Athena tried Aphrodite's room next door.

"Hi," she said when Aphrodite opened up. "Do you know where Artemis is?" Peering into Aphrodite's room, Athena caught a glimpse of her neatly made bed. A plush red velvet comforter stitched with a pattern of little white hearts lay over it, and puffy, heart-shaped pillows had been placed just so, near the head.

Aphrodite looped a wayward strand of her lovely golden hair behind the perfectly-shaped shell of her ear. "Haven't seen her since dinner," she said. Then she eyed Athena closely. "Where were *you* by the way? We missed you."

"I'll explain later," Athena said. "I'm kind of in a hurry right now. Heracles is waiting for me."

Aphrodite arched an eyebrow. "Interesting."

"This has nothing to do with boy-girl stuff," Athena protested quickly.

"Of course not," Aphrodite said knowingly.

Athena sighed. Heracles' cousin wasn't the only one with a one-track mind. But where he was fixated on capturing creatures, Aphrodite was fixated on romance! "See you later," she said, turning to go.

"Come by my room later," Aphrodite called after her. "Maybe I can offer you some pointers."

"Maybe," said Athena, "but I really don't need them, honest." She ran back down the hall and took the stairs two at a time to the main floor. She checked the cafeteria, just in case Artemis was still there, but it was empty. Her stomach growled, and she realized she was starved. Heracles probably was too, since they'd both missed dinner. She grabbed a few apples from a bowl that the eight-armed, octopus-like lunch lady kept filled for late-night snackers. Stuffing them into the pockets of her chiton, she headed out the door.

Athena had only been gone for ten or fifteen minutes, but when she got back outside, Heracles wasn't sitting on the step where she'd left him. She looked around the courtyard, but he was nowhere in sight. Where had he gone?

Just as she was wondering where to look for him, she heard a frantic bleat, and the smallest of Artemis's four deer bounded around the side of the Academy. Moments later, Heracles also appeared. Brandishing his club over his head, he was chasing after the deer.

"Stop!" Athena cried in alarm. Seeing her, the frightened deer bleated again and ran straight toward her. Athena threw her arms protectively around the deer's neck as Heracles skidded to a stop in front of them. He grinned. "Good job," he said, lowering his club to his side. "You caught her!"

Athena scowled at him. "I hate to think what would've happened if I hadn't," she said, eyeing his club.

"Sorry." Heracles gave his club a shake. "I wouldn't really have used it. I only wanted to scare her a little. Just enough to get her away from the other deer."

Athena stroked the deer along her milky-white back. "Isn't she sweet?" she said. "Her name is Delta. She probably would have come right to you if you'd held out a sugar cube or a handful of sweet clover."

Heracles' dark eyes sparkled. "Great idea! I didn't think of that!"

Athena rolled her eyes. It was becoming more and more clear to her that Heracles really needed her counsel. "Anyway," she said. "I thought you agreed to wait until we had Artemis's permission before going after one of her deer."

"I know," he said. "But I thought it would save time if I could catch one while you were gone." He paused. "She did say yes, right?"

"I didn't get a chance to ask," said Athena. "She wasn't in her room."

Heracles reached out to touch the deer, but Delta shied away from him. With a look of disappointment, he let his hand drop to his side. "She's beautiful," he said softly.

Athena nodded. Remembering the food she'd brought, she emptied her pockets. "Here," she said, handing Heracles two of the apples.

"Thanks," he said, munching hungrily. Athena bit off a piece of another apple and held it out to the deer. After sniffing it cautiously, Delta gently took it from her hand.

"I don't suppose we could go ahead and show her to my cousin now, since we have her," said Heracles. "We could return her before Artemis even knows she's missing."

"I'm not so sure that's a good idea," said Athena. But then she reconsidered. First of all, she had no clue where Artemis was. It might take ages to find her. Secondly, it would be dark soon. Already someone had come out to light the torches around the edge of the courtyard. And Heracles had nine labors to go.

"How far away does your cousin live?" she asked, stroking the deer's nose.

"Not far," said Heracles, brightening. "You know where that big market is that's halfway to Earth?"

"The Immortal Marketplace?" Athena and her friends often shopped there.

Heracles nodded. "He lives just south of it. So, what do you think?"

"All right, we'll go," said Athena after a moment. She felt guilty about not waiting to ask for Artemis's permission, but if they could accomplish this task now, they could move on to the boar tomorrow. "We'll get there faster with winged sandals," she said. "There's a basket of them just inside the main door."

"I'm on it," said Heracles. He ran up the granite

steps and was soon back with two pairs. He handed a pair to Athena and they both slipped theirs on. "Whoa!" shouted Heracles, wobbling in surprise as the sandals' straps twined around his ankles. He quickly regained his balance. Then, before the startled deer could even bleat, he swept off his lion's cape and bundled her up in it, so that only Delta's head stuck out at the top. Swiftly he tied the bundle to his club and slung it over his shoulder as if the whole business weighed no more than a carton of nectar.

The deer's eyes looked huge, but she didn't struggle. Athena hoped she wouldn't be too upset by the trip. Already the silver wings on the heels of Athena's sandals had begun to flap. She hovered just off the ground. "Since you're mortal, you'll need to hold my hand to make the sandals work," she told him.

"Really?" Heracles looked at her with eyes as huge as Delta's. "You—um—won't mind?"

Athena considered the question. *Would she?* It wasn't like this was a romantic thing. So there was no reason for either of them to feel nervous about holding hands. "Don't be silly," she said, extending her hand toward his free one.

He wiped his palm against his tunic before he reached for hers. "Sorry," he muttered. "Sweaty."

Athena couldn't help smiling. He was obviously more nervous about holding hands than she was. Not that she had any reason to be, of course! After some fumbling, they finally managed to link their fingers together and were off, skimming their way down the mountain, their sandals barely touching the ground. As they whipped past boulders and trees, Heracles let out a whoop. "Now *this* is the way to travel!" he shouted above the wind.

For a few seconds dense clouds swallowed them up, but then they ducked below the cloud line. "Where to from here?" Athena asked when the high-ceilinged crystal roof of the Immortal Marketplace came into view.

Heracles pointed below and to the right. "Head for Mycenae Hill. It's over there."

Athena nodded. As they neared it, she saw that several stone houses clung to the hillside. Their winged sandals slowed to a hover, and then gently touched down on a narrow road that wound around the hill. Unlinking hands, Heracles gestured to the house at the top, which was larger than all the rest. "That's where my pipsqueak cousin lives."

He set down the bundle with the deer. Delta's head lolled from side to side for a moment as if she was dizzy, but otherwise she seemed none the worse for wear. Athena showed Heracles how to loosen the straps around his ankles and loop them around the silver wings to hold them in place so they could walk normally.

Heracles hoisted the deer again. Delta gave a little bleat, but seemed to enjoy looking all around as he and Athena climbed to the top of the hill. When they reached Eurystheus's house, Heracles rapped sharply on the door. A moment later, a servant answered. "Tell my cousin I've come to see him!" Heracles said loudly.

As the servant disappeared down the hall, Athena heard the sound of something heavy being dragged across a tile floor. She and Heracles followed the sound to a large interior courtyard that was surrounded by columns on all sides. In the center of the courtyard's mosaic floor stood a huge bronze vase that was taller than Athena.

Heracles rolled his eyes at her, then walked up the vase and tapped on it. "You in here, Eurystheus, you little coward?"

A muffled whimper came from inside the vase. "Is that you, Heracles?"

"No, it's *Zeus*," Heracles said with obvious exasperation. "Who else would it be but me?"

Athena couldn't help giggling to herself over Eurystheus being so frightened of Heracles that he'd actually hidden.

"My servant said someone was with you," the voice whined.

"That would be me. Athena," she said, stepping closer to the vase.

Eurystheus was silent for a moment. Finally he said, "The Athena that invented the olive?"

"You got it," said Athena. "Why don't you climb out so I can meet you?"

"No, thanks," said Eurystheus. "And anyway, I don't *like* olives."

Heracles' face turned red with outrage. "You insolent twit!" he roared into the mouth of the vase.

"Well, come on!" came the vase voice. "They're slimy and all dark and small like bugs."

"Show some respect!" Heracles ranted. "Don't you know you're talking to a goddess?"

Athena imagined Eurystheus cowering at the bottom of the vase. She laid a hand on Heracles' arm.

"It's all right," she said. "Not everyone likes olives."

Eurystheus *was* rude, but she was willing to overlook his behavior—for now, anyway.

As if suddenly remembering the purpose of his visit, Heracles said gruffly, "I came to tell you I completed the second and third labors. The Hydra won't be bothering the people of Lerna anymore."

"It can't," added Athena. "It's trapped in its lair."

A muffled grunt of satisfaction came from inside the vase. "And Artemis's deer?"

Heracles lifted the bundle up so that Eurystheus could see the white deer with the golden horns. Startled, Delta bleated.

"Help!" yelped Eurystheus. "Keep it away from me!"

Heracles glanced at Athena with a look that said clearly, *You see what I have to put up with*? Then he placed the bundle back over his shoulder. "Bye, Eurystheus," he said. "We'll see ourselves out."

Once outside the house, Heracles and Athena unlooped the silver wings on their sandals so the laces could twine around their ankles. Holding hands again, they raced through the darkness back the way they'd come. Curling up inside the bundle, the little deer settled down for the ride, like a contented baby on its mother's back.

They had just cleared the clouds when someone called, "Heracles? Athena?" As their sandals slowed to a hover, Athena gulped. Standing on the trail in front of them were Artemis and her brother Apollo. Both had quivers of arrows and their bows. They were obviously just returning from archery practice. So that's why Artemis hadn't been in her room!

Immediately Artemis's three hounds surrounded Heracles. They leaped up, bracing themselves against his legs to sniff at the bundle on his back.

"What have you got there?" Artemis asked curiously. Before Athena could reply, Delta popped her head out. Happy to see Artemis, she bleated with joy.

Dumbfounded, Artemis glanced from the deer to Athena.

"I—that is, *we* can explain," Athena said hastily as Heracles undid the bundle and let the deer escape.

Delta ran to Artemis, who threw her arms around the deer's neck. She glared at Athena and Heracles. "I certainly hope so!"

Hastily Athena explained about Heracles' labors and the time crunch he was under to finish them. "We planned to ask your permission, but we couldn't find you." She lowered her head. "I know it was wrong, and I'm really sorry."

Artemis's expression had softened while Athena spoke. "Well, I guess it's okay. I accept your apology," she said. But her gaze hardened again as she turned toward Heracles. "And how about you? Don't you have anything to say to me?"

"Um—I—" Heracles stuttered. He poked at the ground with the tip of his club. "No harm done, I guess. Right?"

Athena could've told him it was the wrong thing to say. Artemis stiffened, and even Apollo—who *liked* Heracles—was frowning. Ignoring Heracles, Artemis stared at Athena. "Maybe you should be more careful about your choice of friends."

"Oh, hey, wait a second," said Heracles. "If you're going to be mad at someone, it should be me."

"I *am* mad at you, you big lunk!" Artemis exclaimed, throwing her arms wide.

Heracles blinked. "Wow! I get it now. Sorry I'm so dense. You're absolutely right. This whole thing was my fault. If I hadn't talked Athena into it—"

"Oh, never mind," muttered Artemis, interrupting him. As Delta nuzzled her cheek, her anger seemed to drain out of her. "As long as you promise it won't happen again."

"It won't," Athena and Heracles said at the same time. With that, good humor was restored, and all four walked back to MOA together with Delta trotting along at Artemis's side.

7

Gone Hunting

THE NEXT MORNING ATHENA WAS UP AT THE

crack of dawn. It was Saturday, and she'd made

Heracles promise she could accompany him on his

next labor to capture the Erymanthian boar. "But wear

your armor," he'd insisted. "Boars are dangerous."

She smiled now, recalling how he'd laughed when

she'd replied, "Really? I thought those wicked-looking tusks were just a fashion statement!"

Athena dressed quickly in a blue chiton. She tried not to wake Pandora as she rummaged through her closet for her aegis, a large collar with a shield sewn into the front. She'd never had a reason to wear it till now, so she'd stashed it way in the back. As she slipped the aegis over her head, she heard a dog barking from down the hall. It had to be one of Artemis's hounds because they were the only dogs in the dorm. Artemis must have shushed him because within an instant all was quiet again.

Thinking about her friend, Athena felt a rush of gratitude. Though Artemis had been understandably angry last night, she hadn't let her anger get out of hand or last too long. Heracles could stand to take a lesson from her in how *not* to be hotheaded!

Athena stood on tiptoe to reach her helmet on the top shelf of the closet. As she pulled it toward her, it rolled off the shelf. She made a grab for it, but it bounced off her shield and clanged onto the floor.

"Huh? What's that?" mumbled Pandora sleepily as Athena picked up the helmet and shoved it on top of her head.

"Sorry," whispered Athena. "I'll be out of here in a minute. Go back to sleep."

But Pandora was awake now. She yawned sleepily, then sat up in bed. "Why are you dressed like that?" she asked as she pushed back a strand of blue hair that had fallen over one eye. It boinged into its usual question-mark shape. "You going somewhere? It's kind of early, isn't it? Did you forget that it's Saturday?"

"No, I didn't forget," said Athena, choosing to answer only the last question. "I'll be happy to fill you in later, but right now I've got to get going." Dropping to the floor she reached under her bed for a spear that Zeus had given her—"*a present from your mother and me.*" The spear was so long that she hadn't been able to think of anywhere else to store it. Her fingers closed around the spear, and she rolled it toward her. When it was free of the bed, she stood up with it. With the blunt end resting on the floor, the spear was taller than the pointy top of her helmet! It was a formidable weapon, but she hoped she wouldn't actually have to use it.

Glancing over at Pandora, Athena saw that she was already snoozing again. *Good.* She opened the door to their room and sneaked out. Thankfully no one was in the hallway. But as she hurried toward the stairs, the door to the bathroom opened and out stepped Aphrodite. She was wearing a pink satin robe and had a towel wrapped around the top of her head. "What are you doing up so early?" they both asked at the same time.

Aphrodite went first. "I needed to wash my hair. It always takes so long to dry and fix it afterward." Her eyes scanned Athena from head to toe. "So, what's up with the battle gear? I thought we defeated the Titans long ago."

"Ha-ha," said Athena. "I'm going hunting with Heracles."

Aphrodite grinned. "Not for deer, I hope."

Athena's helmet had begun to slide forward. She pushed it back. "You must've talked to Artemis. Did she tell you about the labors?"

"Duh. Naturally. But I would've liked to hear about them from you," she said pointedly, "only you never came by."

"Oops. Sorry about that," said Athena. "By the time I got back I was so exhausted I went straight to bed."

Aphrodite raised an eyebrow. "Just don't spend so much time with Heracles that you forget about the rest of us." Athena seemed to remember Aphrodite giving Artemis similar advice when she was seeing a lot of Orion.

"I won't." Athena gave Aphrodite a quick hug. Which wasn't easy to do dressed in a shield-shirt and helmet. "Later," she said.

Heracles was waiting for her just inside the bronze doors at the entrance to MOA. "Nice armor," he said, nodding his approval. He was carrying his club, of course, and wearing his lion-skin cape. Standing next to him, she didn't feel quite so overdressed.

"Got a ways to travel today. Figured we should use the winged sandals again?" he said, handing her a pair.

"Good plan," she said, noticing that he was already wearing some. She put hers on outside, at the bottom of the granite steps. He was less shy about taking her hand this time, and their fingers laced together as if they held hands all the time.

"We go south," said Heracles as the silver wings on their sandals began to flap.

"How do you know where the boar lives?" Athena asked as they sped across the courtyard.

Heracles smiled at her. "Since he's called the Erymanthian boar, I imagine he lives on Mount Erymanthus."

Well, duh on me, thought Athena. Glancing at him, she said, "You know you're a lot smarter than you give yourself credit for."

"Or maybe you're just rubbing off on me," he said.

They traveled for nearly two hours. When they were almost at the top of Mount Erymanthus, Athena cried, "Look, Kentauroi!" Hiding behind a large boulder, she and Heracles hovered for a few minutes to watch as several of the wild half-human, half-horse centaurs cooked a meal over a fire outside a cave. "I wonder if it would be more correct to call them a *group*? Or a *herd*?" mused Athena.

"How about something halfway in-between," Heracles suggested. "A *gerd*, maybe."

Athena laughed. "Or a *houp*."

As they continued up the mountain, the air turned

colder. Snow covered the ground below their feet and clung to the branches of the trees. They hovered lower again to have a look around. "Boar tracks!" Heracles said at last, dropping down to examine some prints in the snow.

Athena studied the hoof prints over his shoulder. "Are you sure?"

"Yes," said Heracles. "You can tell because the hoof tips are rounded. And this is one heavy beast. See how spread out the toes are?" They followed the boar's tracks as they wound up the mountain. Eventually, they came upon an enormous black beast with a long snout and tusks as sharp as the point on Athena's spear.

Athena elbowed Heracles. "Is that it?"

He nodded. The monstrous boar was breathing

heavily and appeared to be asleep as it lay on its back under a bush with all four of its legs sticking up in the air.

After loosening the ties on their sandals and looping the wings, Athena and Heracles crept closer. Suddenly the boar gave a snort, and its eyes popped open. Athena froze, but Heracles raised his club over his head. "Don't even think about attacking us!" he warned.

The boar stared at Heracles' club in surprise. "Why, I wouldn't dream of it. As you can probably tell," he said, wiggling his hooves, "I'm hardly in a position to mount an attack, even if it was something I was inclined to do. Which it isn't." He paused. "I don't suppose you'd let me sit up? I feel rather silly talking to you with my legs in the air."

"Fine," Heracles grunted, keeping his club at the ready. "But one sudden move, and I'll—"

"Is he always this uptight?" the boar interrupted, winking at Athena as it began rocking side to side.

"I—I don't know," she said uncertainly. Heracles seemed convinced that the boar was dangerous, but she wasn't so sure.

The boar heaved itself up to a sitting position. "You could sit too," he suggested, patting the ground in front of him with a solid-looking trotter.

Gripping his club even tighter, Heracles frowned suspiciously. "Thanks, but no thanks. I prefer to stand."

"I'll sit," Athena said quickly. It just seemed so rude *not* to. Brushing some snow off a rock, she perched on it.

The boar sighed blissfully. "It's so nice to have

company. It gets rather lonely living on top of a mountain. The Centaurs hardly ever make it up this far, and when they do they never stay for long. I don't understand why because I simply adore entertaining guests. I have a huge store of amusing stories I like to share. For example, there's the story about the time I was walking through a forest and came upon an anthill and sat down to watch it. Pretty soon I saw an ant crawl out of a hole at the top, can you imagine? Then another ant crawled out, and it followed the first one down the side of the hill, and a moment later—can you guess?—a *third* ant crawled out of the hill, and after that—"

As the boar droned on and on, Athena glanced over at Heracles. His club had sunk to the ground, and he appeared to have followed it down, till he had fallen asleep using it as a pillow. By the time the boar started to tell about the twentieth ant to crawl out of the anthill, Athena was using her fingers to prop up her eyelids. This was one boring boar! Maybe he *was* dangerous after all. He could probably bore his victims to death!

Hoping to put an end to the thrilling ant story, she leaned forward and cautiously scratched the boar behind one ear the way she did Artemis's dogs. It worked. As he snuffled happily, she reached out with her foot and prodded Heracles awake.

Startled, he grabbed his club again and leaped to his feet. Seeing Athena so close to the boar, a look of alarm came into his eyes. "You leave her alone!" he shouted.

"Calm down," said Athena. She smiled at Heracles. "I was just thinking about inviting our new friend here to go with us to visit your cousin."

"Who, me?" the boar asked with obvious surprise.

"Um—yeah, good idea," said Heracles, relaxing a little as he began to catch on. "My cousin, Eurystheus, *loves* stories."

"He does?" The boar was beaming.

"That's right," said Heracles. "Once he hears that anthill tale of yours, I bet he'll want you to stick around so he can hear *all* of your stories."

"How marvelous!" said the boar, quivering with delight by now. "You probably won't believe it, but I rarely get invited out."

Hiding a smile, Athena said, "Well, you should definitely plan to hang out with Heracles' cousin for a while. Just think, by the time you return home again, you'll have a bunch of *new* stories to tell!"

The boar looked ecstatic. "I bet there are lots of

things this cousin of yours and I could do together. Like maybe we could spend a whole afternoon watching some paint dry. Or waiting for a pot to boil. Or—" He jumped up on all fours. "I'm ready when you are!"

The trip to Eurystheus's house would have taken twice as long if Athena hadn't figured out that she and Heracles could fit the boar's hooves into their winged sandals. The two rode on his back as the sandals carried all three of them down the mountain and across meadows, forests, and towns, until they reached their destination.

Again, Eurystheus was hiding inside his bronze vase when the three of them were ushered into the courtyard. Heracles strode over to the vase and began rubbing it. "Hey! If there's a genie in here, come out and grant me a wish!" he joked.

"Ha!" came the muffled reply. "Very funny."

"I brought you a visitor," said Heracles.

"That olive goddessgirl?" asked Eurystheus, sounding unimpressed.

"Well, yes, but someone else, too." Turning to the boar, Heracles said, "Sorry about this." Then he easily hoisted the boar, which probably weighed a couple of tons, over his head. *Ye gods!* thought Athena. *The boy is definitely strong!*

Eurystheus screamed when Heracles held the boar up to the mouth of the vase.

"If this is the way you welcome your guests, I'm not sure I should have come," huffed the boar.

Eurystheus made no reply. Athena wondered if perhaps he had fainted from fright. But then she heard movement inside the vase and knew that he was okay.

Heracles lowered the boar to the tiled floor. "Don't mind my cousin," he said. "He may not be much of a host, but if you stay right here beside the vase, I'm sure you'll find him a terrific listener."

Athena nodded in agreement. "A captive audience, in fact."

"Be sure and tell him the ant story," said Heracles as he and Athena helped the boar out of the winged sandals and slipped them onto their own feet again. They clasped hands and rose into the air.

Just before they were out of earshot, Eurystheus recovered enough to call after them. "Hope you enjoy your next task, cowboy!" Then he laughed so hard the vase swayed from side to side and almost fell over.

8

Pooped

WHAT *IS* THE NEXT TASK?" ATHENA ASKED

Heracles as the winged sandals whisked them down

the hill from Eurystheus's house. If Heracles could

complete one more task today, that would leave seven

more to finish in six days, improving his chances of

accomplishing them all by next Friday.

Heracles didn't have to consult his list this time.

His face squinched up with a look of disgust. "I've got to clean King Augeas's stable."

"How bad could that be?" Athena asked cheerfully. She was just glad the task wouldn't involve chasing down and capturing another animal. She glanced up at the sky, and saw that the sun was directly overhead. "It's only noon now. We can do it before we return to MOA."

"You think?" asked Heracles.

"Piece of cake," said Athena. "Speaking of which, I'm hungry. You?"

"Starved."

They stopped at an orchard along the way and ate their fill of pears and sweet figs before continuing on. "So, does King Augeus have a lot of cattle?" Athena asked as they approached Elis, the region the king governed.

"Several thousand, I think."

"Whoa," said Athena. "That's a lot!" Cleaning the stables for that many animals could take a bit longer than she had anticipated.

As they entered Elis, an incredible stench filled her nostrils. "P.U.! What is that nasty smell?" she said. Heracles didn't answer. He was staring ahead at some dark brown mountains that stood in a valley between two rivers. "What weird mountains," Athena remarked.

"Um, I don't think they're mountains," Heracles said, shooting her a worried glance. "I think they're piles of dung. As in cow patties. Poop."

"Ye gods!" Athena exclaimed. "Well, that explains the smell."

The stink grew even worse as they touched down by the stables. Looking around at the mess, Heracles wrinkled his nose. "I'm guessing no one's cleaned these stalls in thirty years!"

Athena held her nose. "Good thing we already ate. Kind of takes away your appetite, doesn't it? I'm surprised this stench doesn't reach all the way to Mount Olympus!"

"Might as well get cracking," said Heracles. He found a couple of shovels. Athena pitched in gamely, but after a couple of hours they'd only managed to clear one stall. And though Heracles had done the lion's share of the work, Athena was exhausted. "There must be an easier way," she said, leaning on her shovel. But if there was, she sure couldn't think of it. In exasperation, she exclaimed, "We'd need a *flood* to wash all this away!"

Heracles dropped his shovel. "That's a brilliant idea!"

"Huh?"Athena stared at him in confusion as he left the stable and stalked toward the rushing river on the right side of the valley.

When he reached the riverbank, he began uprooting trees with his bare hands. Athena watched, amazed. With his tremendous strength, it was as easy for him as plucking daisies from a field. Tossing the trees into a pile, he created a dam. Soon the river's waters built up behind it and began to spill over its sides into the valley. Quickly, Heracles built a second dam on the opposite river. Seeing what he was up to, Athena ran for higher ground. Before long, the waters from the two rivers had flooded the stables and washed away the mountains of poop.

Athena and Heracles high-fived in relief. Before they left, they sent out two doves with messages—one bound for King Augeas's castle and the other for Eurystheus—confirming Heracles's accomplishment. Athena hoped the king would be pleased. He couldn't possibly have enjoyed living among mountains of poop!

It was late afternoon by the time they started back to Mount Olympus. When they came upon the little town of Hypaepa, Athena skidded to a stop. "That famous mortal weaver lives here," she said. "A girl named Arachne," she added when Heracles stared at her blankly. He must've been talking to Apollo and the other godboys and missed her conversation with Pheme at the Super Natural Market, she realized. "I want to meet her but I won't stay long. If you want to walk on, I'll catch up in a few minutes." Since he couldn't make the sandals fly without holding her hand, he wouldn't be able to get very far ahead of her.

"'Kay," said Heracles. "Check you later." Swinging his club and whistling off-key, he continued along the road through town.

Not wanting to draw undue attention to herself, Athena transformed herself into an old woman before asking around for Arachne's address. She was directed to a small wooden house at the edge of town. When she knocked on the door, a girl with a big round body, unruly brown hair, and long, thin fingers answered. "Yes?" she said crossly.

Athena peered past her, through the door. She spotted a large weaving loom in the center of the room. Along the walls were neat shelves stacked high with colored yarns. "Are you Arachne?" she asked.

"That's right," the girl said haughtily. "I'm not

surprised you've heard of me. Most people have."

Godness! thought Athena. *This Arachne was certainly full of herself. But perhaps she had reason to be.*

"I know a little about weaving too," Athena said modestly. "I wondered if you might show me some of your work?"

Arachne heaved a great sigh, but opened the door wider. As Athena stepped past her, the girl fanned her hand in front of her nose. "Phew! You stink like a cow pasture, old woman! And you're filthy. Take care you don't touch anything."

She was right, of course. The smell of cow poo still clung to Athena like grapes to a vine. Nevertheless, Arachne's rudeness irritated her. She was about to respond with a sharp retort when she caught sight of the girl's weaving. "Oh! This is lovely work, indeed," she exclaimed, admiring the half-finished scene of a group of women filling urns at a well. The colors were like luminous jewels, and the weave was tight and fine.

"Surely, you must have been taught by Athena herself," she said slyly.

Arachne tossed her head. "No way," she scoffed. "She might be good, but if she ever dared to let others judge our work in a contest, I'm sure I could beat her."

"Show some respect," Athena scolded. "One should not dishonor a goddess!"

"Humph." Arachne flicked her long fingers. "Who are you to give advice?"

"See for yourself who I am!" Athena exclaimed, shedding her disguise and taking her goddess form.

Arachne jumped in surprise. A blush spread across

her cheeks, but then she jutted out her chin and folded her arms. "How like a goddess to try to trick a poor mortal! Still, I stand by my challenge."

"You're on," said Athena. "But if I win, I want you to tell the world who is the better weaver."

"Ditto if I win," said Arachne.

"Deal," said Athena.

They arranged to meet on Thursday morning, in five days' time. Athena had only two afternoon classes that day. She figured she could get away and make it here and back before they started. The two girls agreed to let the women of the town judge whose weaving was better, and Athena departed.

Once on the road again, she changed herself into an owl and flew overhead until she spotted Heracles. Catching up to him, she swooped down and took her goddess form again. They decided to walk the rest of the way to MOA, leaving their sandals loosely strapped. It was a nice evening and the slower pace made it easier to talk.

"How dare she treat you like that!" Heracles roared when Athena told him what had happened with Arachne. It was nice of him to be on her side, she thought. But when he continued to rant and wave his club around, she began to feel uncomfortable and annoyed.

"Let's go back there!" he yelled finally. "I'll knock some sense into her!"

"Stop it!" she said. "Yes, the girl was rude, but you're blowing this way out of proportion."

Heracles stared at her in surprise. "How can you say that? You're a *goddess*! You can't let her get away with such disrespect. Avenge yourself! If you don't, her behavior will only get worse!"

There was some truth in what he said, thought Athena. Perhaps if she'd been more forceful, Arachne wouldn't have been so brazen as to challenge her to a weaving contest in the first place. But if she backed down now, Arachne might think she was afraid of losing the contest. And she wasn't. Well, maybe a little. After all, she was out of practice and Arachne was so skilled she must weave all the time.

She wondered what Ms. Nemesis would advise. Surely not the kind of violence Heracles was suggesting. Her Revenge-ology textscroll might offer some guidance. Maybe she'd browse through it later.

"You know I'm right, right?" asked Heracles, breaking into her thoughts.

Athena frowned. His cocky certainty irritated her almost as much as his eagerness to resort to violence. "I hardly think that knocking someone's head off is an appropriate response to rudeness," she said. "And I expect Ms. Nemesis would agree. Revenge needs to balance the offense to be fair."

"But she's *mortal*," Heracles insisted. "Showing disrespect to a god or goddess is a smiting offense. Ask anybody."

True, thought Athena. *But Heracles was mortal too. So shouldn't he feel more compassion for the girl? Why did he view everything with such certainty?*

"I prefer to keep a cool head and not rush to judgment," she said tartly.

Heracles snorted. "The trouble with you is you're too soft-hearted."

"Now who's disrespecting a goddess?" said Athena. "You're as mortal as Arachne, you know."

Heracles stumbled backward, as if she'd dealt him a blow. She wouldn't be surprised if, because of his superhuman strength, he sometimes forgot his own mortality. "You can smite me if I've offended you," he offered after a moment's pause. "I'm sure I deserve it."

"Oh, don't be so boneheaded," she said tiredly. "I'm not going to smite you or anyone else. Not today, anyway." All she really wanted right now was to be back at MOA so she could take a hot shower and stop smelling of poop.

They walked on in silence for a while. But as they drew near the Academy, Heracles said, "You're right. I *am* boneheaded. I don't mean to be, but I am."

126

"S'okay," said Athena, softening. "You're not bone-headed *all* the time."

Heracles grinned. "I'll take that as a compliment." After a minute he added, "So, I was wondering. Today was fun. How about if you come with me again tomorrow?"

Athena hesitated. She really needed to study tomorrow. Besides, she also had the contest with Arachne to plan for. "What's the next labor on your list?"

Heracles shrugged. "No big deal. I just need to scare off a few birds."

That didn't sound so difficult. Had Eurystheus decided to give Heracles a little break? "Can I decide in the morning?" she asked.

"Sure." He looked a little disappointed that she

didn't jump at the chance, but all he said was, "I'm going to leave early. So if you decide to come, meet me in the courtyard at dawn."

"All right, early bird," she joked, and he laughed.

Then she headed for the dorm—and a shower.

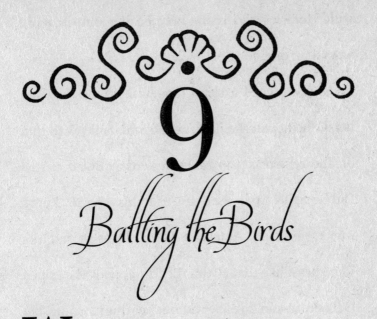

9

Battling the Birds

WHEN ATHENA AWOKE THE NEXT MORNING,
the sun was already up. Well, she'd obviously missed
meeting Heracles. It had to be at least nine o'clock.
Good thing it was Sunday, or she'd be late for school
as well! She glanced over at the empty bed across
from hers. Pandora was probably at breakfast already.
Athena hardly ever slept this late. Yesterday's adventure

with Heracles had really pooped her out, in more ways than one!

As she tugged a clean tangerine chiton over her head, she hoped she hadn't been too cranky with him on the return trip to MOA yesterday. But honestly! Did he really think she'd say yes to his offer to "knock some sense" into Arachne? The girl was mortal, not some beast like that Hydra they'd trapped! She hoped Heracles would do okay without her this morning, but she wasn't all that worried for him. How hard could scaring off a few birds be?

Sitting down at her desk, she reached for her Hero-ology textscroll to begin her homework. Her hero, Odysseus, was on his way home from the Trojan War, and things were getting interesting. Suddenly her window began to rattle noisily. It blew open, and a glittery breeze whooshed in, carrying a rolled-up piece of papyrus. "Art thou Theeny?" howled the breeze. "Most favorite daughter in all the world of Principal Zeus?"

Athena sighed. "Drop it here," she said, holding her hands out to receive the papyrus message. There was certainly no mystery surrounding the sender! There was only one person who called her Theeny. Having made the delivery, the breeze whooshed back out the window.

Athena unrolled the piece of papyrus and began to read.

DEAREST THEENY,

I TRUST ALL IS GOING WELL WITH

YOUR "PROJECT" (WINK, WINK). PLEASE

COME TO MY OFFICE ASAP TO UPDATE

ME ON YOUR PROGRESS. AS YOU KNOW,

I AM COUNTING ON YOU—IN A DOZEN

(GET IT? WINK, WINK) WAYS—TO

SUCCEED.

YOURS IN THUNDER,

ZEUS

(YOUR DEAR OL' DAD)

Beneath his signature, instead of the muscled arm he usually drew (which always looked more like a caterpillar than an arm since he was such a poor artist), he'd actually scratched a row of *X*s and *O*s. Talk about pouring it on thick! And she certainly couldn't accuse him of subtlety. A *dozen* ways? Could there be a more obvious reference to Heracles' *twelve* labors? Had her dad forgotten he'd never told her about them? Parents were so hard to figure out sometimes.

Sighing, Athena set the message on top of her desk and rummaged in a drawer for a Breakfast of the Gods power bar. She was starving. She hadn't eaten a thing since the fruit she and Heracles had gorged on yesterday afternoon, just before cleaning King Augeas's disgusting stables.

After peeling off the wrapper she gulped the bar down in three quick bites. Then she glanced at the half-dozen textscrolls on top of her desk. She hadn't touched any of them in the two days since Heracles' arrival, and it seemed to her that they scowled at her reproachfully. She had assignments for two classes and an exam to study for before tomorrow. Surely,

Zeus wouldn't expect her to abandon her studies to help Heracles. Perhaps he was just clueless about how much study time it took to keep up a straight-A average. Instead of going to see him right away—*as soon as possible* didn't necessarily mean *now*, did it?—she picked up her textscrolls and headed for the library.

After she finished her Hero-ology assignment, she picked up her Revenge-ology textscroll. She unfurled it and started to read Chapter 3: The Nature of Justice. Then, remembering her encounter with Arachne, she consulted the Table of Contents and skipped ahead to Chapter 6: Dealing with Disrespect. She scanned the chapter until a particular sentence snagged her attention: "When a mortal insults a god or goddess, retribution is required."

Athena frowned, furrowing her brow. Retribution

was *required*. But *had* Arachne insulted her? She wasn't really sure. Certainly the girl had been rude and cross and haughty. Skimming to the end of the chapter, she found a table titled "Responding to Mortal Insults: Acceptable Retributions." What followed was a list of things mortals could be turned into. It included such things as toadstools, small animals, bugs, trees, flowers, and astrological signs. Athena studied the list thoughtfully.

At lunchtime she gathered up her textscrolls and walked down the hall to the cafeteria. Aphrodite, Artemis, and Persephone were already there eating. Usually Persephone wasn't around on the weekends since she lived at home with her mom, instead of in the dorm with the rest of the goddessgirls. But she sometimes hung out at MOA when her mom was busy at her flower shop in the Immortal Marketplace.

Athena smiled her thanks and took the bowl of nectaroni and cheese the eight-armed lunch lady handed her, then went to join her friends. She would've had to be wearing a blindfold to miss the curious glances they gave her when she sat down. Even Artemis's dogs stared up at her, but they were probably just hoping for some of her nectaroni and cheese. With her fork halfway to her mouth, Athena stared back at the other three goddessgirls. "What?"

"We know all about the labors," Aphrodite said. "But you've never told us why you're helping Heracles with them." Athena put down her fork and opened her mouth to reply. But Artemis spoke up first.

"He probably asked her to," she said. "And she was too nice to say no!" Her dogs looked at her nervously.

"No" was a word they didn't much care for. "He's taking advantage of her because he knows how smart she is and needs her help."

"Nonsense," said Persephone. She looked at Athena. "Hades thinks Heracles must like you. Otherwise he would've asked some of the godboys for help instead." She paused. "And I think you're helping because you like him, right?"

Again, Athena tried to speak, but she was interrupted. "Of course Heracles likes her," said Aphrodite. "She's perfect for him, and—"

Athena held her hands up in front of her. "Stop!" Eyeing each goddessgirl in turn, she said, "Yes, I like him. And I think he likes me. But that doesn't mean we're getting married, for godness sake. Give it a rest!" After this declaration, she glanced uneasily around the room to make sure the nosy Pheme wasn't near. Fortunately she was several tables away, sitting with Pandora and Medusa.

Artemis nodded. "Believe me, I understand completely. Consider the subject rested."

"Good." Athena calmed herself and got back to her nectaroni. After all, her friends' curiosity was understandable. They didn't know Zeus had asked her to offer Heracles some guidance. Of course, it wasn't really true that Zeus had asked her to help Heracles with his labors. Still, his letter this morning had certainly *hinted* at that. But the main reason Zeus had asked her to guide Heracles was because he was worried the boy would lose his temper and get into trouble. And she'd never tell anyone that. It just wouldn't be fair to Heracles!

"Well, I still think Hades is right. Heracles must *really* like you," Persephone insisted. "Or he wouldn't have asked for your help. After all, any godboy at MOA would've jumped at the chance to get in on the excitement."

Athena wished she could tell her that helping had been more her idea (and Zeus's), than Heracles'. At the beginning, anyway.

Aphrodite nodded, blotting the pink lip gloss she'd reapplied after finishing her nectar. "Godboys do love to show off in challenges, especially physical ones."

"But would a guy ask a girl he *like*-likes to help him clean up mountains of cow poop?" Athena asked. "That's what Heracles and I did yesterday."

Her friends wrinkled their noses in disgust. "Euuww," said Persephone. "Are you serious?"

Athena nodded, though in truth Heracles had been reluctant to ask for her help with *that* task. She'd *volunteered*. Despite Aphrodite's protest that it wasn't a fit topic to discuss during a meal, Athena told the other goddessgirls all about King Augeas's filthy stables and how Heracles finally managed to clean them. She also told them about the many-headed Hydra, the boring boar, and Heracles' cowardly cousin. The only part of her adventures of the last two days that she left out was her stop in Hypaepa to see Arachne. She was a bit embarrassed about that whole thing. What would her friends think of her if they knew she'd agreed to that silly contest? Competing with a mortal? It really *was* an undignified thing to do.

As the four girls were leaving the cafeteria, Pheme jumped up from her table and dashed toward them.

"Athena! Wait up!" she shouted. Catching up to them, she said, "Guess where I just came from?" Her glossy orange lips parted in a big smile.

Artemis rolled her eyes. "That's easy. The cafeteria."

"Well, yes," said Pheme, frowning a little. "But I meant *before* that."

"Artemis was joking," Athena said. Honestly, sometimes Pheme was a bit dense.

"Oh!" Pheme smiled again. Without waiting for any more guesses, she blurted out, "I just got back from Hypaepa!"

Athena groaned inwardly. What rotten luck! "Well, we have to get going—" she began, hoping to hurry her friends away.

"Wait a sec. That's where that mortal weaver lives, right?" said Aphrodite. "The one who made that fabulous chiton you were wearing at the Super Natural Market on Friday. What was her name? *Acne?*"

"Arachne," corrected Pheme.

Aphrodite nodded. "I remember now. Same as the sewing shop in the Immortal Marketplace."

"Did you order another chiton from her?" Persephone asked. "Is that why you went to Hypaepa?"

"Yes," said Pheme. "And while I was there, she told me about her contest with Athena next Thursday, and—" Her words puffed above her head, where everyone could see.

"Gotta run," Athena interrupted quickly. "Love to hear more about your trip later, Pheme." She pushed open the cafeteria door, then glanced over her shoulder at her startled friends. "Coming, everyone?"

With puzzled looks on their faces, they followed her outside.

"Contest?" Artemis asked. "What's that all about?"

Aphrodite stood with her well-manicured, pink-polished hands on her hips. "Come on. Give. You're holding something back from us!"

"I didn't mean to, it's just—" Athena stopped, unsure how to explain.

Persephone touched her arm lightly. "You don't have to say if you don't want to."

"Nonsense," said Aphrodite. "Of course she does. We're her best friends."

Athena sighed. "If Pheme already knows about the contest, so does half the school. Or they will soon enough, anyway. I guess I'd rather you heard about it from me than from her. C'mon."

Upstairs in Aphrodite's room, Athena and Persephone sank onto Aphrodite's bed, while Aphrodite and Artemis took the opposite bed. A little embarrassed, Athena traced her fingers over the small white hearts stitched into the bed's plush velvet comforter as she told her friends about her encounter with Arachne.

"The nerve of that girl!" Artemis exclaimed when she finished. "I wish I'd been there. I would've nocked an arrow in my bow and . . ." She mimed the action, pretending to draw a silver arrow from the quiver slung across her back. "Zing!" she shouted with glee. "Right in the kisser."

Ye gods! thought Athena. *Artemis sounded just like Heracles! Even supposing that Arachne's speech and actions* could *be considered an insult, shooting a mortal in the face with an arrow was* not *on the list of Acceptable*

144

Retributions. Her dismay must have shown because Artemis started to laugh. "I'm only kidding!" she said. Then she scowled. "But you really shouldn't have let her get away with challenging you like that!"

"Don't I know it," Athena said, hugging a heart-shaped pillow to her chest.

Aphrodite shot Artemis a warning look. "What's done is done," she said. "Besides, Athena will win the contest."

"That's right," Persephone said. "Arachne may weave well, but no one could match Athena's skill."

Athena was glad they had such confidence in her. She only wished she felt as sure of her weaving prowess as they did. When she returned to her room a while later, she took out her loom. Though she knitted a lot, she hadn't done any weaving since she'd started school at MOA. She was so out of practice that her fingers felt clumsy as she stretched parallel threads across her loom, then began to pass her yarn over and under them. Still, she kept at it, staying in her room until dinnertime. As she worked, her mind wandered to Heracles, and she wondered how things were going for him today.

When she got downstairs to the cafeteria, she saw he was back, sitting at a table with Apollo, Hades, Poseidon, Ares, and several other godboys. The cafeteria was once again buzzing with the news of his latest "adventure." From what Athena could piece together while standing in line for a salad topped with some of the delicious olives she had invented, the "few birds" Heracles had referred to yesterday were no twittering songbirds. They were vicious death-dealing birds of prey with armor-piercing beaks and wings that shot arrows!

"Come on, Heracles," Apollo was urging as she neared the boys' table with her tray. "Tell us how you defeated them again."

As Heracles began retelling his tale through a mouthful of yambrosia stew, the godboys hung on his every word. Athena could feel his eyes on her as she walked past, but she pretended not to see him. To tell the truth, she was glad to see he hadn't been pecked to death. But she found it a bit annoying that he got to play the hero while she was dealing with a challenge from an upstart mortal girl—who just might beat her!

"You think you've got problems!" Aphrodite said in a huff when Athena sat next to her. "I'm never going to speak to Ares again!"

"What happened?" Athena asked, spearing an olive.

Yum. Heracles' cousin was crazy. Olives were delicious!

Persephone swallowed a sip from a carton of nectar. "She and Ares got into another argument."

Aphrodite's on-again, off-again crush was a never-ending topic at lunch, and Athena listened sympathetically to Aphrodite's love woes as she munched on her salad. Although she had no advice to offer, Persephone and Artemis had plenty, most of it conflicting.

"Ares was probably just in a bad mood," Persephone soothed. "If you wait a while, I bet he'll apologize."

"He's a jerk," said Artemis while feeding bits of her sandwich to her three dogs. "You're better off without him."

Athena knew she shouldn't be glad for Aphrodite's

troubles, but it was a relief to let someone else be the center of attention for a change. As soon as she finished her salad, she excused herself and got up to leave.

"Sorry. Gotta go," she heard Heracles say to his many admirers at the same time. She wondered if he'd decided to leave just because she was leaving. Sure enough, he caught up with her outside the cafeteria. "Hey, I missed you today," he said.

Athena raised an eyebrow.

He blushed. "Your help, I mean. I missed your help."

She sniffed. "Why would you need my help when you have your club?"

He cocked his thumb back toward the godboys. "My fan club you mean?"

"No."

Heracles' brow wrinkled in confusion. "Oh!" he

said after a pause. He clapped a hand over the club he held against his shoulder. "You think I used this on those birds today?"

"Well, didn't you?" she asked accusingly. Even though she now knew that the birds he'd faced weren't any sweet flock of songbirds, she hated to think he'd killed them.

"I thought about it," Heracles admitted. "But even as they dove toward me, I asked myself: 'What would Athena do?'"

"Really?" she said, unsure if he was teasing.

He looked a little hurt. "I'd never lie to you, Athena," he said solemnly. He stared at her for such a long moment that she started to squirm under his gaze. Finally he said, "So, I figured out how I could scare off the birds without actually harming them."

"How?" she asked.

"Used my brains. Just like you would've. I picked up a couple of rocks and—"

Athena sucked in her breath.

"—and I slammed them together like cymbals. *Crash!* You wouldn't believe the racket they made!"

"And did the noise drive the birds off?" she asked eagerly.

"More or less."

Athena cocked her head. "More or less?"

"Well, a couple of the bolder ones just wouldn't leave, so I—!"

"No! Don't tell me!" she said, fearing the worst. "I'll just imagine to myself that you caught them in a net."

"Yeah, that probably would've worked," Heracles said, not quite meeting her eyes.

Athena decided to change the subject. "What's next on the list? Something that involves capturing or scaring off more animals, no doubt."

Heracles grinned. "I have to capture a Cretan bull."

"In Crete? But that's so far away!" Athena exclaimed.

He nodded. "I'll have to sail there."

She thought about telling him that she invented the ship, but he probably already knew that. And anyway, she didn't want to him to think she was bragging.

"I'm leaving tonight," he added.

"But what about school?" Athena asked. "You can't possibly get back by tomorrow morning for class."

Heracles shrugged. "I'll have to skip." He paused. "I—I don't suppose you'd go with me."

Athena hesitated. She'd never skipped school a day in her life! On the other hand, Zeus *had* asked her to keep an eye on Heracles. But she needed to prepare for her Thursday contest with Arachne, plus there was a quiz tomorrow and she was still behind in her schoolwork. Besides, Heracles had done just fine on his own today. "I'm sorry," she said finally. "I can't go. I've just got too much to do here."

Heracles' shoulders slumped.

"I bet one of the godboys would go with you," she suggested brightly.

"Maybe," he said, but he didn't seem very enthusiastic about the idea. After an awkward silence, they said good-bye.

"Good luck!" Athena called after him as he left. "Will you let me know when you're back? Just sneak into the girls' hall and shove a note under my door if it's late."

"'Kay," Heracles mumbled. She could tell he was disappointed that she wasn't going with him. It made her feel guilty. But it was also flattering. Still, she wasn't going to skip class and ruin her grades over any boy, even one she liked!

Once he'd disappeared upstairs, she set off for the library again. After she did more homework, she planned to study some art textscrolls. She hoped they would give her some ideas for scenes to create in her weaving. As she shoved through the library doors, she tried not to think of all the things that could cause a ship to flounder and sink, such as high winds and jagged rocks. Or of how dangerous bulls could be.

10

Missing Heracles

REVENGE-OLOGY CLASS ON MONDAY AFTER-
noon just wasn't the same without Heracles. Athena
missed him, and though she was sure she knew what
his response would have been, she would've enjoyed
sparring with him about the day's question: Should
one always avenge an injury? Led by Medusa, the
class had been tilting toward yes in their responses, so

Athena was pleased when Ms. Nemesis interrupted the discussion to address the class. "I'd like you all to consider this," she said, as her wings fanned out majestically behind her. "It often takes more strength to forgive an injury than to insist on having one's revenge."

Athena agreed, but she raised her hand to ask about the difference between an *injury* and an *insult*, since the latter *required* retribution according to her text-scroll. Before Ms. Nemesis could call on her, however, there was a knock at the door and Mr. Cyclops, the Hero-ology teacher, stuck his head in the room. "Excuse me," he said. The humongous eye in the middle of his forehead focused on Ms. Nemesis. "May I speak with you a minute?"

"Certainly," Ms. Nemesis told him. She stepped into

the hallway, and as soon as the door clicked shut, everyone started goofing off. A folded-papyrus air-bird whooshed past Athena's desk, thrown by someone in the back, and someone else started humming the latest song by Apollo's band. Medusa slipped out of her seat. Planting herself in front of Athena's desk, she leaned toward her and asked, "Where's your boyfriend today?" Her green hair writhed and hissed, the snakes flicking their forked tongues in Athena's face.

Athena scooted back in her chair, just out of their reach. "I assume you mean Heracles," she said coldly. "I know it's useless to tell you this, but he's *not* my boyfriend. And the only reason he's not here is because he had something very important he needed to do today."

"Off on another of his little adventures, huh?" said Medusa. "I bet you wish you were with him."

"He asked me to go, but I—" Athena clapped a hand over her mouth. Goddessgirl of wisdom? Hardly! How stupid of her to let herself be drawn into this conversation! Medusa was sure to relay this little tidbit to Pheme, and then rumors about her and Heracles would be flying all over the school—if they weren't already.

"Oooh," said Medusa, pretending to swoon. "I think someone's in *lo-ove*. Heracles and Athena sitting in an olive tree. K - I - S - S - I - N - G." Two of her snakes lunged forward to form a heart shape around Athena's face.

Athena itched to throttle them. She clenched and unclenched her fists, and just for a moment, she could totally understand Heracles' hotheaded reactions. But how could she respect herself and lay claim to any wisdom at all, if she couldn't set a proper example for him and for others—even when it was hard? Taking a few deep breaths, she silently counted to ten to regain her composure.

Sending Medusa a sweet smile, she simply said, "Cute." Medusa stomped back to her desk. She was obviously frustrated at not having made Athena mad. Athena smiled inwardly. *Score!*

But when Heracles didn't show up in the cafeteria at dinnertime, she grew worried. What if a Siren's song had lured him to a watery death? What if the Cretan bull had fatally gored him? Sure, he was strong, but he was also mortal. She silently scolded herself for not accompanying him.

A few of the godboys already knew Heracles had skipped to go to Crete. Apparently he'd told them about the bull before he left and now everyone knew, including Athena's best friends. Unfortunately he'd ignored Athena's advice about taking a godboy friend along.

"Apollo and I offered to go with him," Hades said, as he helped himself to the ambrosia pudding Persephone had been too full to finish. "So did Poseidon and Ares, but he turned us all down. I hope Principal Zeus is okay with him cutting classes to do these labors. Otherwise, Heracles could get kicked out of MOA."

Persephone smiled up at him. "You should talk."

Hades blushed. He often skipped classes, usually because he was needed in the Underworld. Luckily, Zeus had overlooked his absences so far.

After dinner, Athena went to study in her room. She also worked on her weaving, though she still hadn't decided on a design for the contest on Thursday. Around eight o'clock, Pandora stuck her head in the door. "Mind if I spend the night with Pheme?" she asked. "We'll be up late working on a project for Beauty-ology class, if that's okay?" Even when something didn't need to be a question, Pandora couldn't seem o help making it one.

"No problem," said Athena as she tightened a thread on her loom. "Have fun." Then she added, "But don't believe everything Pheme may tell you—especially if it's about me!"

Pandora laughed. "Do you really think I believe everything she says?"

After she left, Athena kept working at her loom,

experimenting with various patterns as she wove colored threads back and forth through the looped threads. It was good to have something to occupy her hands and mind, but every few minutes she glanced toward the door, hoping to see a note from Heracles appear under it. When a knock finally sounded, she jumped up in relief. She practically tripped over her loom in her haste to open the door.

"Oh, it's you," she said dully, when she saw who was standing there. "Come in."

Aphrodite and Artemis exchanged a look. "Gosh, thanks," said Aphrodite. "Nice to see you, too."

"We know it's late," Artemis said, "but we saw your light on. Since you're usually in bed by now, we wondered if everything's—"

"Heracles isn't back yet," interrupted Athena.

"What if he's hurt, or—or *worse*?" She sank onto her bed with her head in her hands.

As Artemis shut the door, Aphrodite hurried to sit beside Athena. "Calm down," she said putting an arm around her. "I'm sure Heracles can look after himself."

"But Zeus asked me to keep an eye on him!" Athena cried. "If anything's gone wrong, it'll be all my fault!"

"Keep an eye on him?" Artemis echoed, as she plopped down on Athena's other side.

Athena clapped a hand over her mouth. "Oh, no. I wasn't supposed to tell anyone that. But it's true! My dad wants me to report to him about what Heracles is up to, but I still haven't done it. How can I tell him I let Heracles go off to Crete without me? On the other hand, how am I supposed to go to class, get all my own work done, *and* watch over Heracles at the same time?"

Aphrodite frowned. "I don't get it. Surely Principal Zeus wouldn't want you to ignore your schoolwork to traipse after Heracles. Maybe you should tell him about the labors. He probably doesn't know."

"Oh, he knows," said Athena. "I'm sure of it." He'd hinted broadly enough about them in yesterday's note. In fact, since he'd been speaking through the oracle that Heracles consulted, he'd basically *assigned* him the twelve labors. "What I don't get is why it's so important to my dad that Heracles do all those tasks."

"Why don't you ask him?" asked Aphrodite.

Athena sent her an *are you kidding* look. "If he wanted me to know, he would have told me. You know he doesn't like his orders being questioned."

Artemis nodded. "If I were king of everything in sight, I guess I wouldn't either."

"This is probably a silly question," said Aphrodite, "but are you sure Heracles isn't already back?"

Athena nodded. "He said he'd let me know when he got in."

"But what if he forgot?" said Artemis. "Maybe he was exhausted from the travel and corralling that bull and everything. For all we know, he could be sound asleep in bed!"

"You think so?" asked Athena, feeling a burst of new hope.

"Only one way to find out," said Aphrodite. "C'mon."

A few minutes later, the three goddessgirls sneaked down the hall and upstairs to the boys' dorm on the fifth floor. Right away they heard music. Athena, who played the flute, recognized the sound of the kithara—a seven-stringed lyre—and the double-reeded aulos.

"Apollo and Dionysus must be practicing," whispered Artemis. "That's their room," she said, motioning to a door on their left. The two godboys were part of a band called Heavens Above that played for all the school dances.

The girls tiptoed farther down the hall. Outside of Ares and Atlas's room stood a suit of armor. As the girls drew near, it clanked into the middle of the hall and held up a shield to block their path. "Halt!" it said in a deep voice. "No man shall pass!"

"Humph," Aphrodite said with a frown. "Ares must have put a spell on it." The two of them were still not on speaking terms. "We're not men, we're *women*," she said to the armor. "*Goddessgirls*, that is, so step aside!"

The armor swayed back and forth, appearing uncertain how to respond. Then, as if remembering some former training, it lowered its shield and bowed, creaking, at the waist. "Pardon me, fair ladies," it said, "please continue thusly." Then it clanked back to its original position outside Ares and Atlas's room.

The girls scooted past the armor and continued down the hall. When they were directly across from the boy's bathroom, the door swung open. Out stepped Poseidon, clad only in a towel wrapped around his waist. He squealed when he saw them, holding his trident in front of him with one hand (which was no help as a shield), and tightening his grip on his towel with the other. Water dripped from his light turquoise skin and puddled on the floor at his feet.

"What are you doing here?" he said in an embarrassed squeak.

"Looking for Heracles," said Athena. "Which room is his?"

Still gripping his trident and his towel, Poseidon jerked his chin toward the right. "Next door down."

Artemis had been staring at Poseidon ever since he appeared. Finally she asked, "You shower with your trident?"

"Um—well—yeah." Blushing, Poseidon sprinted across the hall and disappeared into the room he shared with Hades—whenever Hades wasn't spending the night in the Underworld, that is.

There was a large piece of papyrus tacked to Heracles' door. Big block letters spelled out a message: "Gone to Crete. Back later." He'd mentioned once that he didn't have a roommate yet, so Athena didn't worry about waking anyone but him when she knocked lightly. No answer. She put her ear to the door, but heard nothing from inside. Her shoulders slumped. "He's not here. Let's go."

On the way back down to the girls' dorm, Aphrodite said to Athena, "I noticed earlier that you've set up your loom. Getting ready for the contest?"

Athena nodded, but she didn't want to admit that she was still stuck for a good design.

"We'll be glad to go with you to Hypaepa on Thursday," said Artemis, glancing at Aphrodite.

She nodded. "We've talked about it, and Persephone said she'll come too."

Artemis grinned. "It'll mean missing Beauty-ology class," she said. "But that's a sacrifice I'm willing to make."

"I appreciate it," said Athena. "But I think I'd rather go alone."

"You sure?" Aphrodite asked.

"Yes," said Athena as they reached her room. "But thanks for the offer. It's really sweet of you."

Artemis shrugged. "Suit yourself. But if you change your mind, let us know."

"I will," Athena promised.

"And try not to worry too much about Heracles," Aphrodite said. "He's bound to turn up by morning."

Artemis nodded in agreement. "The trip to Crete probably just took longer than he thought it would."

"Yes, you're probably right," said Athena as they all said good night. Even so, after Aphrodite and Artemis left, she considered waking Zeus to tell him about Heracles. She abandoned the idea only because her dad was always horribly cranky when he didn't get enough sleep. But when Heracles didn't show up in

Revenge-ology the next day, Athena summoned her courage and marched down the hall to Zeus's office.

All of Ms. Hydra's heads were busy when she arrived, but the administrative assistant waved Athena toward Zeus's open door. When Athena peeked inside, she saw a large scale-model of a temple sitting smack in the middle her dad's desk. But no Zeus.

"Hello?" she called.

His big red-haired head popped up from behind the model. "Theeny! About time you came to see your dear ol' dad. I sent you a message two days ago. Didn't you get it?" He ducked his head again. The model faced him, and he was fiddling with something on his side of it where she couldn't see.

Athena gulped. "Yes, but I had a lot of schoolwork, and—"

171

"Never mind," Zeus interrupted. "You're here now. Sit. Sit." Taking the same green chair with the scalloped back that she'd sat in the last time she was there, Athena rolled her eyes. The way he told her to sit always made her feel like he was commanding a pet dog.

"Is that a model of the temple I saw plans for last Friday?" she asked, when he didn't speak right away. What was he doing back there anyway?

Zeus nodded enthusiastically and turned the model around, so she could see the front. Judging from the small size of the windows and doors in relation to the overall building, the temple was going to be huge. It was surrounded on all sides with soaring columns, covered with lots of marble and gold, and out in front there was a pedestal with a giant statue of Zeus himself holding a thunderbolt.

"Awesome, isn't it?" he said, his face glowing with excitement. "I told the architect I wanted something that would make mortals fall all over themselves to worship me the minute they saw it."

"That ought to do it," said Athena, admiring the model.

Zeus eyed it critically. "You don't think it needs more geegaws?"

"Geegaws?"

He waved his hands around. "You know. Maybe a bunch of wreaths over here, bows over there, banners, beasts, towers. More stuff like that stuck here and there."

"No, I think it's nice as it is," said Athena tactfully. The building's design was clean and tasteful, the exact opposite of Zeus's ideas. She noticed a dozen or so small, moveable doll-like figures set around the statue of him, and realized he must've been playing his own version of "house" with them, moving them around the statue of himself, pretending they were Greeks coming to worship him. *Ye gods! Sometimes he acted like an overgrown kid!*

Zeus nodded. "You're probably right. Besides, it's almost built. Just the artwork and sculpture left to consider." Looking in one of the windows, Athena noticed the blank areas on the walls and the vacant pedestals. Abruptly Zeus shoved the model aside and, leaning on his elbows with his hands steepled together, he peered at her keenly. "So how's our boy doing?"

Athena squirmed in her chair. "Oh, well. I—I don't know exactly. He went to Crete yesterday. He should've made it back by now, but—"

Zeus's brows shot up to form two big, angry *V*s.

Both of his palms hit the desk, making everything in the room jump, including Athena. "WHAT?" he thundered. "You let Heracles go off to Crete on his own? Without telling me? After I specifically asked you to watch out for him?"

Athena cringed. "I know, I know. It's just that I didn't want to bother you. I thought he'd be back sooner than this. I'm sorry."

Grunting suddenly, Zeus slapped the side of his head and got that familiar, spacey look in his eyes that meant Metis was talking to him. "Yes, you're right, it might have been wiser of me to choose someone other than Eurystheus to come up with the list of labors," he admitted, with a mix of irritation and reluctance in his voice. "And yes, I suppose I should've reviewed the list myself before it was given to Heracles, but I didn't expect—" Metis must have interrupted because he sighed, listening again. "I know it was an awfully short deadline, but the temple will be—" His voice trailed off and his expression turned sneaky as he glanced at Athena. "We can talk more about this later, Metis," he growled.

"The temple will be what?"Athena asked when he "hung up" on Metis.

"Huh?" Zeus looked at her blankly.

"The temple will be *what*?" she repeated. "You didn't finish your sentence. And were you talking about the temple where Heracles went to consult the oracle? Or the one being built in your honor? Or some other temple?"

Just then Ms. Hydra poked two of her heads in at

the door, interrupting them. Was it her imagination, or did Zeus look relieved?

"A letter just arrived from Hermes' Special Delivery," the assistant informed him. A rolled-up piece of papyrus tied with a wide red ribbon wriggled as it struggled to escape her grasp. As soon as she released it, it flew on tiny wings to land on Zeus's desk.

Zeus removed the red ribbon and unrolled the papyrus. After scanning it quickly, he said, "It's from Heracles." Then he began reading aloud from it:

DEAR PRINCIPAL ZEUS,

SORRY FOR MISSING SCHOOL YESTERDAY.
AS ATHENA MAY HAVE TOLD YOU BY
NOW, [And here Zeus raised his shaggy

head to give Athena a long, hard look.]

I'VE BEEN IN CRETE, WRANGLING A

BULL. TODAY I MOVE ON TO THRACE

TO CORRAL SOME HORSES, AND THEN I

WILL BE OFF TO NORTHERN AFRICA TO

RUSTLE SOME CATTLE BELONGING TO A

GERYON. YEE-HAH!

Ye gods! thought Athena. *A real* Geryon? She and

her friends had battled one of them not long ago in

the Forest of the Beasts, but that had only been a fake

one. Real Geryons were terrifying one-headed, two-

armed, three-bodied, four-winged, six-legged beasts

with vicious talons, slimy green lips, and extremely

bad breath that was even worse than that of the black

sheep of Ms. Hydra's family!

Zeus read on:

ANYWAY, I EXPECT TO RETURN TO

MOA THURSDAY MORNING. AND I

PROMISE TO STUDY DOUBLE-TIME TO

MAKE UP THE WORK I'M MISSING IN MY

CLASSES IF ONLY YOU'LL ALLOW ME TO

STAY AT THE ACADEMY.

WORSHIPFULLY,

HERACLES

Zeus looked a little guilty as he finished. He must have finally realized he'd set Heracles an impossible task, expecting him to complete all twelve labors in one week and still remain in school and keep up with his classes. Though she was relieved to know Heracles was okay, Athena couldn't help feeling a bit hurt that he had sent Zeus a message to let him know what was going on but hadn't bothered to contact *her*. Didn't he think she was worried about him? It was pure luck that she happened to be here when his letter arrived. Otherwise, she'd be in the dark!

Shaking off her hurt feelings, she did some quick calculations. If all went well, Heracles would have only three labors left to complete when he got back Thursday morning. She wished she knew what they were. If only she didn't have her contest with Arachne. She didn't want to miss his return!

"Couldn't you give Heracles an extra day or two to finish the twelve labors?" she suggested to Zeus, though, having heard his one-sided conversation with her mom, she figured she knew the answer.

Zeus shook his giant head from side to side. "Once a god's words have been uttered through an oracle, they can't be changed."

"Oh," said Athena. "I was afraid of that."

Zeus tapped his fingertips together. Sparks flew out from between them and landed on a pile of papers on top of his desk. "I can't tell you how important Heracles' success is to me, Theeny," he said.

Nodding, Athena leaned over and began blowing on the smoldering papers to prevent them from bursting into flame. It was truly a wonder his office hadn't burned down by now.

"I need for you to continue helping him," Zeus was saying. "After he returns, I want you to stick to him like a flea on a lion until he completes every last one of those labors."

Athena didn't like being compared to a flea. Still, one didn't quibble with the King of the Gods over his choice of similes, even if he was one's dad. "Okay," she said, "but—"

"No buts about it," interrupted Zeus with a frown. Unlike last Friday, he seemed in no mood today to plead for her consent. He was *ordering* her now. She'd been about to mention her commitment to Thursday's weaving contest, but now she thought better of it. If Zeus was so set on her helping Heracles, his reasons had to be important. Maybe she should try to find a way to wiggle out of the contest.

Zeus's eyes went spacey again, and he thumped his hand against the side of his head. "All right, Metis. Take it easy. I'll tell her!" Rolling his eyes at Athena, he said, "Your mother wants you to know that we love you dearly, and that no one else will ever take your place in our hearts—no matter how strong they are or how skilled at battle. You've got other skills that are—um—just as important and useful."

"Other skills?" Athena repeated.

Zeus paused, listening to Metis again. Finally he said, "Art skills, for example." He waved a meaty paw in the air. "You're good at inventions and all that sewing stuff—you know, like *weaving*—"

"Gotcha," Athena said quickly. Luckily the lyrebell sounded just then. She jumped to her feet. "Guess I'd better go, huh? Don't want to be late for class!"

"Yes, go," said Zeus, somewhat distractedly. From the way he kept shaking his head, it appeared that Metis was still yakking at him. "Don't forget what I said," he called to her as she hurried out the door.

About how he and her mother loved her dearly? Athena wondered, *or about sticking to Heracles like a flea on a lion?* It was obvious that Zeus took pride in Heracles' strength and battle skills, she thought as she ran down the hall to her next class. She didn't mind that, not really. Well, maybe she did, actually. Just a little. She wished Zeus hadn't brought up her weaving. It was nice to know that her mom and dad loved her regardless of her skills, but she wanted them to be *proud* of her too. As proud as Zeus was of Heracles. She simply *couldn't* skip the contest now. If she did, it would be like admitting she thought she would lose, and that would not make her parents proud. She couldn't let a mere mortal best her at a skill for which she was so famed. That wouldn't be wise at all!

Still, how could she be in two places at once?

11

The Contest

ATHENA GOT UP AT THE CRACK OF DAWN on Thursday morning to finish choosing her yarns. The previous night, she'd finally come up with an idea for a design, and she knew it was a good one. She moved around her room quietly, trying not to wake Pandora. Just as she was about to leave she realized she'd need something to eat along the way. She ran to her desk to grab a couple of breakfast bars and stumbled into her chair. "Ow!"

She froze as Pandora's eyes flew open. "Huh?" she mumbled. "Did you say you like me, Poseidon? Really . . . ?" Her roomie mumbled something else that Athena couldn't quite make out—though it sounded like a question, of course—then she promptly rolled over and fell back to sleep.

After pocketing the snacks, Athena picked up her bag of yarns and left, closing the door soundlessly behind her. At the end of the hall, she donned a pair of winged sandals, then skimmed down the marble staircase, whizzed through the bronze doors, and was off to Hypaepa.

As she descended Mount Olympus, she wondered if she should have taken her friends up on their offer to accompany her after all. She'd been afraid their presence might make her feel nervous, but now she wasn't so sure. They could have cheered her on! She felt tired and anxious. She'd slept poorly during the night, going over and over her design and fretting about today's contest. Though she told herself there was no way she could lose, a tiny bit of doubt, no bigger than an olive pit, had worked its way into her mind.

Athena coasted to a stop just outside of town. Loosening the straps at her ankles, she looped them around her sandals' silver wings, then walked the rest of the way. When she knocked on the door of Arachne's small wooden house, the girl called out, "Let yourself in. I'm busy!"

Humph, thought Athena as she turned the knob and pushed open the heavy door. She'd never met anyone with such poor manners—mortal *or* immortal!

Arachne's long, thin fingers were already at work stringing her loom. "Over there," she grunted, cocking her head toward a second loom. Athena went over to the loom and inspected it. Though it wasn't as fine or as sturdy as her own back at MOA, it would do. She opened her bag and took out several balls of yarn. After cutting off long lengths of thread from each, she tied, stretched, and looped the threads from top to bottom to create columns of threads called the warp.

Once both looms were strung, the girls each set to work, passing new threads over and under the warp, then pulling the threads tight at the end of each row. Few weavers could have matched the rhythm and pace of their nimble fingers. As the design she had planned began to emerge, Athena's confidence grew. Instead of one big scene, she'd divided her design into sections, each with a different, but related, scene. Every thread was in exactly the right place, and her colors were as vibrant and true as the masterful murals that adorned the walls of MOA.

When her tapestry was almost finished, she glanced up and was surprised to see that a group of women had quietly entered the room. They were the judges, of course, and stood watching, just inside the door. Athena caught the eye of one of them, an older woman with white hair and gnarled hands. The woman lowered her gaze and bowed reverently. Now *that* was the kind of respect a goddess expected from mortals!

Several minutes later, at almost the exact same moment, Athena and Arachne declared their tapestries done. With a sly, self-satisfied grin on her face, Arachne stepped away from her loom. Athena wondered what she had woven, but the women who had come to judge the contest had moved between the two looms to examine both tapestries, and Athena couldn't see over their heads. Awed exclamations, aimed equally at the work of both girls, began to fill the room: "Incredible! Beautiful! Exquisite!"

But then some of the judges admiring Arachne's work began to laugh awkwardly, darting glances at Athena. "Superb work, as usual, Arachne," said the older woman who had bowed to Athena, "but hardly a fit subject."

"May I see?" asked Athena, overcome with curiosity. The judges drew back to let her through. Arachne's tapestry sparkled with lush colors, and its flawless weave was every bit the equal of Athena's. But the picture! It showed a crazed-looking Zeus dancing around in pain as a fly (Metis, no doubt!) buzzed around his head. A badly aimed thunderbolt was stuck in his foot, and another had set the hem of his tunic on fire.

At first Athena was too shocked to speak. Then her eyes narrowed and her cheeks grew hot. She glared at Arachne. Perhaps realizing the enormity of what she'd done, the girl's face turned pale with fright. "How dare you!" Athena exclaimed. Erupting with fury, she pounced on Arachne's tapestry and ripped it to shreds. Then she stomped on it for good measure as Arachne stood trembling and the women stared on in horror. Making fun of *her* was one thing, but Athena couldn't allow this girl to dishonor her parents!

Consumed with anger, she now turned on Arachne herself. "With your mockery of my parents, you've doomed yourself forever to spin empty, colorless threads!" Reaching out, she touched the girl. Immediately Arachne's head and body began to shrink and her ten long, thin fingers began to change into eight spindly legs. When the change was complete, Arachne, now a spider, scurried up the nearest wall and began to weave a fragile web. As if afraid of what Athena might do next, the judges all fled the house, even the older woman who'd been properly respectful and therefore had nothing to fear.

Her wrath spent, Athena cut loose her tapestry with its six spectacular, vibrant scenes. She rolled it up, stuffed it into her bag, then headed back to Mount Olympus on winged sandals. As towns and trees and boulders rushed past, her mind began to calm. Thinking about what had just happened, she could scarcely believe what she'd done! It seemed to her now that she'd let anger carry away her reason. She'd lashed out in a way that was more like Heracles than like her, using violence to solve her problem.

Was his influence rubbing off on her instead of the other way around? She felt sure he'd have approved of her actions if he'd been there to see what happened. Yet had she been so wrong? Arachne *had* insulted her parents, after all. Retribution was required. She'd been within her rights to destroy the girl's tapestry and turn her into a spider. Still, she couldn't help wondering if, instead of delivering justice, she'd simply been vengeful. How did one tell the difference? At times like these, being a goddessgirl was really hard!

It was lunchtime when Athena reached MOA. As she entered the cafeteria she spotted Pheme. The goddess-girl of rumor obviously had some delicious gossip today, for she dashed from table to table, words puffing from her lips faster than winged sandals could fly. Athena's stomach sank. Had the news of what she'd done in Hypaepa reached Pheme's ears already? But a moment later she discovered that Pheme's news was about Heracles, not her. Somehow the orange-haired goddess had learned the contents of the letter he'd sent Zeus.

Athena breathed a sigh of relief. No doubt Pheme—and through her everyone else—would learn of Arachne's fate soon enough, but for now Athena could relax. Even her friends held off asking her about the contest in their eagerness to tell her what they'd heard about Heracles that morning.

"The Cretan bull was so huge and savage that no one on the island could catch him," Persephone reported, gesturing wildly. "But Heracles managed to seize him by the horns. Then he tossed the bull into the sea and rode him all the way back to land."

With her spoon full of yambrosia stew almost to her mouth, Athena looked at Persephone in surprise. Those details hadn't been in the letter! "Is Heracles here?" she asked, glancing around the room. She hadn't seen him when she entered the cafeteria. She'd just assumed he hadn't yet returned.

Aphrodite shook her head. "He was, but he left about an hour ago after telling everyone his adventures."

Oh, flute loops, Athena huffed. Before she could ask if Aphrodite knew where he'd gone, Artemis spoke up. "Did you hear how he captured the man-eating horses and tricked a Geryon so he could steal its herd of red cows?"

Athena was surprised to hear the admiration in her voice. It sounded like Heracles' daring deeds had finally won her over. And considering all the stuff he'd done, who wouldn't be impressed by his strength and courage? "Yes, I did hear something about that," she said hurriedly. "Does anyone know where he is now?"

"He told Hades he had to go pick some magic apples," said Persephone. "It's another of his labors. Atlas went with him."

"He did?" Though Athena had been the one to suggest that Heracles ask the godboys for help, she'd secretly liked that he seemed to prefer her help. She liked feeling special—the only person at MOA whose advice Heracles valued. "Did he ask about me?" she asked with pretended nonchalance.

Aphrodite and Artemis exchanged a look. "I'm sure he must have," Aphrodite said at the same time that Artemis shook her head no.

Athena tried not to feel too hurt, but her disappointment must've shown because Persephone changed the subject. "So tell us about the weaving contest. I bet you astounded everyone!" she said brightly.

With a wry smile, Athena said, "Yes, I guess you could say that." And then she told them what had happened.

When Heracles returned that evening he was in high spirits. Even from her room four floors up, Athena could hear him singing loudly and off-key as he swaggered across the courtyard at the front of the school. Still a little hurt that he hadn't waited for her to return from Hypaepa so she could accompany him on his next labor, she held back for a few minutes. But eventually she gave in and raced downstairs.

Unfortunately, almost everyone else at MOA had heard him coming and had run down to meet him too. There was already an admiring crowd around him at the bottom of the granite steps by the time Athena got outside. Juggling three magic apples, Heracles exclaimed, "You wouldn't believe what I had to go through to get these! They're only grown in the Garden of the Hesperides on a magical tree with golden bark and golden leaves." He kept the students spellbound as he told them how he'd tricked a shape-shifting sea god into revealing the well-kept secret of the hidden garden's location.

"Where's Atlas?" someone asked after a while.

Heracles grinned. "I left him holding up the sky."

The godboys in his audience laughed, but Athena frowned. *Holding up the sky? What kind of joke was that to play on poor Atlas?* "Don't you think you should go back for him?" she asked.

As if just noticing she was there, Heracles smiled at her. "He looked like he was having fun," he said good-naturedly. He rubbed the back of his neck. "But I guess I should."

"We'll go get him," offered Ares and Poseidon.

Once they left, the crowd began to disperse and Heracles found Athena. "Hi. Good to see you again." He smiled at her, almost shyly.

"You too," Athena said, softening toward him. "But you could have sent me a note, like you did Zeus, when you realized you were going to be late."

Heracles raised an eyebrow. "You didn't worry about me, did you?"

"'Course not," Athena lied.

He cocked his head toward her. "You sure?"

"Well, maybe a little," she admitted.

Suddenly he turned serious. "You don't ever have to worry about me," he said, his dark brown eyes holding her gray ones. "I've never yet met a situation I couldn't handle." He held out one of the magic apples. "Eurystheus can have the other two, but I got this one for you. It was the prettiest."

"Thanks," she said, touched by his generosity. The apple was perfectly round and shone like a miniature sun. As she took it from him, their hands touched. To her confusion, Heracles blushed. Why? After all, they'd held hands several times while wearing the winged sandals. Pretending she hadn't noticed the rosy glow that had spread over his neck and face, she said, "So, now you're done with the tenth task, right?"

"Actually, the apples were the eleventh labor," he said.

"Eleventh?" Athena repeated. "Did I count wrong? I thought you had two more tasks to complete."

"Well, I skipped—uh—postponed the ninth one," he said, his blush deepening. "The other labors were easier, so I'll get back to that one later." Before she could ask what the ninth labor was, he rushed on, "You're friends with Persephone, right? Do you think you could get her to keep Hades busy for a couple of hours tomorrow morning?"

"Why?" asked Athena.

"I need to borrow his dog for a little while."

Athena's eyes widened. "Cerberus? Let me guess. You have to show him to Eurystheus. For the next-to-last labor."

Heracles grinned. "You got it."

Was it possible he'd already forgotten how upset Artemis had been when they'd taken her deer without her knowledge? "Wouldn't it be better to ask Hades' permission instead of trying to take Cerberus behind his back?" Athena suggested.

Heracles rubbed his chin, thinking. "But what if he says no?"

"Just give it a shot," Athena urged. "I thought you guys were getting to be friends."

"Yeah. Well, okay. If you think it's best, I'll ask him in the morning." He yawned. "Sorry. It's been a long few days. I could sleep for a week!"

"Oh! I shouldn't have kept you talking," said Athena. "You're exhausted!"

"That's okay. I *wanted* to talk to you," Heracles insisted. Still, he didn't protest when she gently took his elbow and propelled him up the steps of the academy.

"Wait a second," he said, as they pushed through the bronze doors, "I forgot to ask about your weaving contest."

Athena sighed. "Don't ask."

"Uh-oh. What happened?"

"I'll tell you tomorrow."

"No," he said stubbornly. "Now!" Pulling her down beside him, he sank onto the marble staircase that led up to the dorms. He refused to budge until she told him the entire story.

"You turned her into a spider?" he said when she'd finished. "Awesome!"

"You don't think I was too harsh?" she asked.

"No way. Arachne deserved it!"

His words were a comfort, but Athena still had doubts about whether she'd done the right thing. Heracles' view of the world was so simple. For him right and wrong were easy to distinguish, like black and white. Not so for her. She saw things in shades of gray, which meant some things were sort of right and sort of wrong. If she'd learned one thing from her encounter with Arachne, it was that all gods, herself included, could act as rashly as mortals when anger ran away with them. Perhaps true wisdom meant realizing and accepting that.

Snort! Her thoughts were interrupted when Heracles sagged across her lap. He was snoring! She gave him a gentle push.

"Wha—?" he exclaimed, his eyes popping open. Seeing where he was, he quickly straightened. "Sorry. I didn't mean to—"

"Come on," Athena interrupted softly. "You need to get upstairs." They climbed the steps together and said good-bye at the entrance to the fourth-floor dorm.

Once she was back in her room, Athena couldn't sleep. Instead, she began to weave a new tapestry, continuing with the same subject she'd chosen for her contest with Arachne. She smiled to herself, imagining how surprised Heracles would be when she showed him her work, for he had inspired it. She was weaving scenes from all of his labors. While the contest tapestry showed scenes from Heracles' first six labors, the new tapestry would illustrate the last six. She would show Heracles riding the Cretan bull across the sea, corralling horses, herding the Geryon's red cattle as the monster roared with fury, and juggling the golden apples.

She wished she'd remembered to ask Heracles what the ninth labor was—the one he'd skipped. He'd implied it would be harder than all the other labors, but she couldn't imagine anything more difficult than the tasks he'd already completed! She would add scenes for the ninth and twelfth labors after Heracles completed them tomorrow. And if he needed her help with that mysterious ninth labor, she'd do all that she could to ensure his success.

12
Last Labors

ATHENA GOT SO INVOLVED IN HER WEAVING that night that even after Pandora came in and went to bed, she continued working. Naturally, she overslept the next morning—the second time that week!—and had to skip breakfast. After gobbling down a couple Breakfast of the Gods power bars from her rapidly diminishing supply, she hightailed it down to the main floor. She'd just pulled some textscrolls from her locker when Persephone raced up to her, a look of distress on her naturally pale face. "Hades just sent me a note!" she said, waving the sheet of papyrus clutched in her hand. "There's trouble in the Underworld!"

Athena gulped. "Is Heracles involved?" She was pretty certain she knew the answer.

Sure enough, Persephone nodded. "At breakfast this morning he asked if Hades would let him borrow Cerberus."

"But Hades said no?" Athena guessed.

Persephone nodded again. "Heracles seemed okay with the refusal, but Hades followed him when he left the cafeteria, just to be sure."

"Let me guess," said Athena. "Heracles went down to the Underworld and tried to *sneak* Cerberus out."

"Uh-huh. When Hades caught up with him, Heracles was trying to attach horns to Cerberus's heads."

Athena gave her a puzzled look. "Horns?"

Persephone shrugged. "It was a disguise, I guess. He was trying to make Cerberus look like a three-headed goat!"

"As if that would fool anyone," said Athena, groaning. "So now Hades and Heracles are the ones butting heads, I bet."

Persephone nodded. "And I'm worried someone will get hurt!"

Given Heracles' size and strength, it would most likely be Hades, thought Athena. *No wonder Persephone was worried! Well, if ever there was a good reason for skipping class, surely this was it.* She shoved her textscrolls back in her locker and slammed it shut. "Let's go sort this out."

Quickly, they each shape-shifted into birds—Athena an owl, and Persephone a dove—and winged it down to the River Styx, where they shape-shifted back into themselves. "We have to go by boat," Persephone told her. "That's the only way."

Having visited the Underworld to see Hades many times by now, Persephone knew the grizzled old ferryman, Charon. "Who's your friend?" he asked her, as he reached down to pull the two goddessgirls aboard his boat.

After Persephone made the introductions, Charon dipped his pole into the river and shoved off. "So I suppose you heard about the fireworks going off on the opposite shore," he said grimly. "All that growling and barking really upset my first load of passengers, and it wasn't Cerberus making the noise!"

Persephone and Athena looked at each other worriedly. "Can't he go any faster?" Athena whispered. Persephone shook her head. "No, and don't ask."

Unfortunately, Charon had overheard her. "The living are always in such a hurry. That's why I prefer the dead. They're in no rush at all."

Eventually, their boat bumped into the far shore, and Athena and Persephone jumped off. "Thanks!" they called to Charon as he pushed off again to return to the other side.

A dank, gray mist made it hard to see what lay ahead as they rushed down a marshy path. But Athena could hear the boys yelling up ahead. She almost lost a sandal in the muck, and the strong smell of rotting grasses in stagnant water made her feel like gagging. As she had expected, the Underworld was a gloomy place.

But then the mist cleared, and they came upon fields and fields of tall stalks topped with pretty white flowers. "Asphodel," Persephone informed her matter-of-factly. "It's what the dead eat—the *shades*, that is."

Interesting, thought Athena, inhaling the flowers' sweet scent. She would've liked to have had time to look around—to maybe meet a few shades since this was her first time here. But she and Persephone were on a mission! At the far edge of the second field of asphodel they came upon the boys.

Heracles was waving his club around like he intended to use it. But on what or on whom? Hades was nowhere to be seen. And Cerberus lay some distance away, with his three heads on his paws and his snakelike tail curled around him. He seemed to have wisely decided to stay out of the boys' argument.

"Can't clobber what you can't see, can you, Heracles?" Hades' voice taunted, surprising both goddessgirls.

"He must be wearing his cap of invisibility," Persephone whispered to Athena. "He told me about it once, but said it's only meant to be used during times of war."

"Close enough," Athena whispered back as Heracles thrashed at the air with his club.

"Come on, fight fair! Show yourself!" he shouted.

"Stop it right now!" Athena yelled. Startled, Heracles spun toward her.

"You, too, Hades!" Persephone called out. "This is ridiculous!" Hearing her voice, Cerberus's heads popped up and his snakelike tail began to wag joyfully. Leaping to his feet, he bounded over to Persephone and licked her face with all three of his tongues.

As Heracles lowered his club, Hades whipped the magical cap off of his head and became visible. Athena eyed the two of them sternly. "Let's talk this out."

"I tried that already," said Heracles, glaring at Hades. "My club is mightier than talk. The best way to settle this is by fighting."

Athena folded her arms across her chest. "No!" She pointed to the ground. "Sit! Sit!" She sounded just like her dad!

But it worked. The boys sat. So did Cerberus.

"Shake hands," she said.

Cerberus held up a paw. "Not you," said Persephone,

ruffling his fur. She pointed to the boys. "Them."

Looking a little sheepish now, Heracles reached out his hand to Hades. After some hesitation, Hades shook it.

"That's better," said Athena. Looking at Heracles, she said, "Did you explain to Hades why you wanted to borrow Cerberus?"

"Yes. Because I need to show him to my cousin."

Hades frowned. "That's hardly a good reason for taking him out of the Underworld. Cerberus is a working dog. He's got a job to do here!"

Everyone glanced at Cerberus. The dog had rolled onto his back and was writhing back and forth in the grass as Persephone scratched his stomach. "I can see that," Heracles said drily.

Athena couldn't help smiling a little. "Did Heracles

explain to you that borrowing Cerberus is his twelfth labor?" she asked Hades.

"Yes," said Hades. "But I don't like the idea of Cerberus being part of this, regardless of what some oracle said. What's the point of all these labors anyway?"

Athena didn't tell him it was something she'd been wondering about too. Zeus must have a reason—beyond his stated aim to see if Heracles truly belonged at MOA—but whatever it was, he certainly hadn't let *her* in on it. And surely it was something important! "Look, you know that Heracles' cousin got to decide what the labors would be, right?" Athena said to Hades. "They weren't Heracles' choosing."

Hades nodded.

"Well," said Athena. "Since this is the *twelfth* of

the twelve labors, it must be the biggest, most difficult and impressive task he could think of." She paused to let that sink in.

Hades didn't say anything, but she could tell he was listening intently now.

"Eurystheus obviously sees Cerberus as one of most fearsome creatures ever, right up there with the Hydra, the Cretan bull, and the Geryon. Why, it's practically an honor that Cerberus was included in the labors." Athena didn't mention that cleaning King Augeas's stable had also been on the list of labors and hoped that Hades hadn't heard, or at least wouldn't remember, about that one.

Luckily her words seemed to sway him. "Really?" He looked at Heracles, who nodded. Hades went silent for a moment, as if deep in thought. Then he said to

Heracles, "If I did let you borrow Cerberus—"

"Yes?" said Heracles eagerly.

"*He'd* have to agree to it. I mean, you'd have to take him without force."

"Sure, okay," said Heracles.

"And as a sign of good faith," Hades continued, "you'd have to leave your club with me until you returned Cerberus to the Underworld."

"Impossible!" Heracles roared. He hugged his club to his chest.

"Ye gods," Athena said. "You're as attached to that club as Eurystheus is to his vase!"

A wounded look came into Heracles' eyes. "It's not the same thing."

Athena stared at him. "Isn't it?"

Heracles looked down at his club. "Well, all right,"

he said with a sigh. "If I have to." Cradling it like a baby, he placed it in Hades' arms.

"Whoa!" exclaimed Hades. He staggered forward, almost losing his balance as his arms dropped with their heavy load. "Not exactly light, is it?"

Heracles fixed him with a solemn gaze. "Do you promise to watch over my club and keep it safe?"

To his credit Hades didn't laugh. "Cross my heart and hope to die," he said soberly. Since Hades was immortal, this wasn't much of an oath, but Heracles accepted it.

Still, Cerberus didn't seem too eager to leave the Underworld, especially not with someone who had tried to stick horns on his heads. He snarled and snapped when Heracles tried to pick him up.

"Try these," said Hades, pulling a handful of dog

treats out of his pocket. With the help of the treats, Heracles was finally able to coax Cerberus into going with him. Persephone and Athena accompanied them onto Charon's boat, but Hades stayed on the bank by the river to wait for Cerberus's return. As they shoved off, Heracles stared longingly at his club, which Hades still held. "Maybe I could just—"

"Forget it," Athena interrupted. "The club stays in the Underworld. Be glad Hades made the deal at all."

Heracles pouted a little, but she held firm. When they reached the other side, he and Cerberus bounded off for his cousin's house.

By the time the girls arrived back at MOA, they'd missed their morning classes as well as lunch. "See you later," Athena called to Persephone. Then she hurried off to Revenge-ology.

Heracles eventually showed up toward the end of class, without Cerberus, and with his club. "Sorry I'm late," he told Ms. Nemesis. She only nodded and asked him to take his seat. Athena wondered why she let him off so lightly, especially since he hadn't been in class for a whole week, but then she realized that if all the students knew about Heracles' labors by now, the teachers must know too. Probably Zeus had told them to excuse his absences.

Heracles gave Athena a thumbs-up before he sat down. Smiling big, he pointed to his club. They didn't have a chance to talk, however, until class was over. "Thanks for your help with Cerberus," he said as they left the room together.

"Everything went okay?" she asked.

He nodded.

"Did Eurystheus hide in his vase?"

Heracles laughed. "He was more terrified of Cerberus than of all the other creatures put together! You should've seen how proud Hades looked when I told him. I think Cerberus was happy about it too."

"So," said Athena, "only one more labor to go. That ninth one."

Heracles glanced at her uneasily, shifting from one foot to the other. "Yes."

"It must *really* be hard since you put it off till the end," she said as they drew near the lockers.

He sighed. "It is. *Very* hard. Very, very hard. Very very very—"

"Okay, I get it. But maybe I can help."

Gesturing toward a bench across the way, Heracles said, "Could we sit for a sec?"

223

Athena nodded, and after they sat down, she leaned toward him. "I'll do everything I can to help you succeed. You know that, right?"

Hope sparked in his eyes. "You promise?"

"Of course," said Athena. "Just tell me what the task is."

Not quite looking at her, he opened his mouth and then closed it and then tried again. Eventually, he shook his head. "I—I can't say it. I've just got to do it."

"Okay!" said Athena. What could possibly be harder than poop, bulls, killer birds, and everything else he'd already done, she wondered?

"You'll help me?" he said with a strange, determined glint in his eye. Was it her imagination, or had he moved closer to her along the bench?

She nodded. "I said I would. So—"

"Thanks," he interrupted. And before she could say another word, he closed his eyes, puckered his lips, and swooped toward her.

Startled, she turned her head. His kiss landed on her cheek. Athena jumped up from the bench. Her face felt like it was on fire. "Ye gods. W-why did you do that?" she demanded. But before he could say a word, she burst into tears. She wasn't sure why. His kiss was just . . . so unexpected!

He jumped to his feet, looking upset. "Athena, I'm—"

Too embarrassed to listen, she turned to flee . . . and ran smack into Medusa and Pheme.

"Now *that* was an interesting little scene," said Medusa, wearing an even bigger smirk on her face than usual. Pheme's eyes were sparkling as she stared across at Heracles. She was obviously relishing the choice bit of gossip she'd just been handed.

Athena glanced back at him.

"Athena!" he called. "Sorry if I misunderstood. I—"

"Leave me alone!" she yelled. Her humiliation complete, she backed away from all three, then turned and ran upstairs to her room.

13

Finding the Favor

ATHENA THREW HERSELF ONTO HER BED
and buried her face in her pillow, sobbing with
embarrassment and—and something else, too—*confu-*
sion. Heracles' attempted kiss had turned her world
upside-down. Suddenly she wasn't as sure of her feelings toward him as she'd thought. *Did* she like him as

more than a friend? He *was* cute, and she did enjoy being with him. How did one know for sure?

Aphrodite and Persephone thought he liked her. But what if he'd only been taking advantage of her to help with his labors, as Artemis had once suggested? She wished she knew what he really thought of her. She punched her pillow. It was too much to sort out. If only she could stay in her room and never come out!

But she couldn't, of course. The lyre bell would sound any moment. So after drying her tears, she grabbed another power bar (though she was starting to get sick of them), and dutifully trudged downstairs to attend her afternoon classes. She peeked around every corner first, though, making sure she wouldn't run into Heracles. She wasn't ready to deal with him yet. Ignoring the curious glances cast her way and the whispers swirling around her, she kept her nose buried in her textscroll during class.

Her three best friends were waiting to meet her as she left the room.

"Did you—?" Athena began.

"Yes, we've heard the rumors," Aphrodite said as they steered her past staring students. Persephone nodded gravely. "That's why we're here."

"We'll make sure no one bothers you," Artemis added. Her three friends surrounded her like a protective shield as they started down the hall.

As the girls neared the marble staircase, Heracles appeared. "Athena," he called out. "Can I talk to you? Please?" He seemed oblivious to the snickers that broke out from several small groups of students that happened to be passing by just then.

Athena's friends scowled at him.

"Get lost, Lionboy," barked Artemis. "You've done enough harm for one day." Growling deep in their throats, her hounds bared their teeth.

Aphrodite arched an eyebrow. "Can't you see your attentions aren't welcome?"

"It would be best to keep your distance for a while," Persephone advised him.

"I'm asking Athena," Heracles said stubbornly. Ignoring the other girls' scowls he took another step toward her. "Won't you please talk to me, Athena?"

She wanted to refuse him, but wouldn't that undermine what she'd been trying all week to show him—that it was best to solve a problem by talking it through? Besides, there was such misery in his eyes! "All right," she said at last.

"Are you sure?" asked Aphrodite.

Persephone studied Athena's face. "This is what you really want?"

"Maybe we should stay with you," said Artemis. "Just in case he tries anything."

Athena waved her friends away, smiling a little at her friend's ferocity. "I can handle it. But thanks, you guys."

"We'll be in my room if you need us," Aphrodite called back over her shoulder as the three goddessgirls started upstairs.

"I'll be up soon," Athena replied. She turned back toward Heracles. For the first time, she noticed that two large bags dangled by their handles from his club.

Her heart squeezed in her chest. "Are you leaving?" she asked, trying to keep the panic she felt out of her voice.

He shrugged, looking uncomfortable. "Zeus is sending me back to Earth."

"But why?" She didn't want him to go!

Heracles stared down at the floor. "I told you yesterday that I hadn't yet met a situation I couldn't handle. Well, now I have. I totally messed up on that ninth labor. I was supposed to win the favor of a strong girl. Since you're the strongest girl I know, I tried to figure out how to make you like me. I thought kissing you would do it. But I—I made a mistake." He glanced up again. "I'm sorry. I really do like you Athena."

She didn't need to be the goddessgirl of wisdom to know he was speaking the truth. *Tell him you like him, too,* she thought, but her tongue lay like a heavy stone in her mouth.

"I told Zeus the truth about what happened,"

Heracles continued, blushing a little. "Since I failed to complete all the labors, it's only fair that I should leave Mount Olympus and remain mortal." He paused. "But I couldn't go without thanking you for your help—even if you just did it because Principal Zeus asked you to."

Now it was Athena's turn to blush. "Did my dad tell you that?"

Heracles nodded.

"He asked me not to tell you," she said. "But the truth is, I was *glad* he asked me to help you. She glanced at him shyly. I—I enjoyed it."

Heracles nodded. "Thanks for saying so." As he shifted his club and his bags to his other shoulder, Ms. Nemesis's words came flooding back to Athena: "It often takes more strength to forgive an injury than to insist on having one's revenge." If she let Heracles go now she could avenge her embarrassment and confusion over the presumptuous kiss. But was that what she wanted? She smiled, remembering that day in Ms. Nemesis's class, when he'd dropped his club on his foot. When Ms. Nemesis had asked if he was all right, he'd replied, "Nothing broken. Except my pride."

Well, her "injury" was no worse. In her heart, she'd already forgiven him. And as they stood there, an idea began to form in her mind. Perhaps she could fix things so he could stay at MOA!

"How soon are you leaving?" she asked.

"Hermes is supposed to come for me in his chariot in an hour. I'm going to wait in the library."

She nodded. "There's something I need to do. But then I'll—"

"You're busy," he interrupted, backing away. "It's okay. We can say good-bye now. I understand."

"No, you don't," she said reaching out to lightly touch his arm. "Meet me in Principal Zeus's office in forty-five minutes, okay? Don't leave MOA without doing that. Promise?"

His brow wrinkled, but he nodded. "'Kay."

Smiling, Athena ran upstairs to her room. The tapestry on her loom was complete except for one last scene. Her fingers flew as she wove that final scene into the design. When the tapestry was finished a half hour later, she removed it from the loom and rolled it up like a scroll. Then she grabbed her first tapestry— the one she had woven for the contest—stuffed both weavings into a bag, and left her room.

Aphrodite flung open her door before Athena

could even knock upon it. Inside, Persephone and Artemis jumped up from Aphrodite's pillow-strewn bed where they'd been playing Grecian checkers. "What happened?" they all asked at the same time.

Athena told them everything Heracles had said. When she finished, Persephone sighed. "Heracles did act rashly. But he also apologized. I think he sounds kind of sweet, just like Hades."

"So do you believe him?" Artemis asked. "You think he was being honest?"

Athena nodded. "I do."

"The strongest girl he knows," repeated Aphrodite. Her eyes sparkling, she hugged a heart-shaped pillow to her chest and sighed with delight. "Oh, he likes you all right. What a shame he has to leave!"

"Maybe he *doesn't* have to," said Athena. Pointing

to her bag, she told her friends her plan. "Heracles is going to meet me in Dad's office in just a few minutes. Will you all come too? I could use the support, and I might need some witnesses."

The three readily agreed, and minutes later all four goddessgirls trooped into Zeus's office. If he blamed Athena for Heracles' failure, she couldn't tell, though the new scorch marks she spotted on the furniture and walls suggested that he was *not* in the best of moods. The girls had just pulled up chairs around his desk when Heracles arrived too.

"You still here?" Zeus growled, rising from his golden throne.

Heracles' face reddened. He started to mumble an apology and to back away, but leaping up from her chair, Athena waved him closer. Still holding on to her

237

bag, she leaned over Zeus's desk. "There's still time for Heracles to complete his remaining task before this day ends, isn't there?" she asked.

Zeus frowned. "Yes, but I thought—" Daring to interrupt her father, Athena turned toward Heracles again. "Please kneel before me."

A look of confusion came into Heracles' eyes, but he humbly knelt at Athena's feet. As her dad and her friends looked on, Athena withdrew the two tapestries from her bag. "With this gift, I—a strong goddessgirl— bestow my favor," she said, handing Heracles the rolled-up weavings.

"I don't understand," he said, taking them. "What are these?"

"Tapestries," said Athena. "Unroll them."

"Oh," he said, looking pleased as understanding

dawned. "You made them? For me?"

She nodded.

"OPEN THEM ALREADY!" boomed Zeus, and everyone jumped. He shoved a pile of papers, magazines, and empty bottles of Zeus juice off his giant desk, making room. Heracles unfurled the two tapestries on top of the desk, and everyone crowded around. Athena couldn't help feeling proud as the dozen scenes she'd woven were greeted with delighted *ooh*s and *ahh*s.

"They're—they're wonderful!" Heracles exclaimed, carefully examining each one. "I can't believe you did this! All twelve labors! No one's ever given me anything so nice!"

At his praise, Athena felt an unfamiliar fluttery feeling inside her stomach. She found herself wondering what it would've been like if she *hadn't* turned her head when Heracles had tried to kiss her. If her plan succeeded and he stayed, maybe she'd have to ask Aphrodite for some pointers after all!

"Is that boy hiding in a *vase*?" Aphrodite asked, pointing to a scene showing Heracles holding the Erymanthian boar up to the mouth of the vase while his cousin crouched inside. Athena and Heracles nodded, laughing.

"That's my exceedingly brave cousin, Eurystheus," said Heracles.

"Is that my deer?" gasped Artemis, gazing at another scene Athena had woven that showed Delta peeking out of the bundle on Heracles' back. "She's so beautiful! And she looks real enough to pet!" Artemis ran her hand over the stitches, looking awed.

"Look, there's Cerberus!" Persephone said, as she examined the second tapestry. "And here you are at the end," she said to Athena, "handing the tapestries to Heracles! As Zeus looks on."

They all turned to look at her dad. Zeus had been uncharacteristically quiet all this time, but now he clapped a hand on Athena's shoulder. She jumped a little as electricity zapped her. "This is fantastic, Theeny!" he said. "Even better than I hoped for! Of course, I didn't *know* you would weave these when I asked you to—um—when you decided to help Heracles, but—" He stopped talking as his eyes grew spacey. "Yes, Metis, dear," he said. "Theeny's tapestries *are* works of art! And no, I wasn't going to just assume she'd let me copy them. I was going to ask."

"Copy them?" asked Athena.

Zeus smiled, looking at her with evident pride. "With your permission, I would like to have my architect copy your designs to adorn my new temple!" He waved toward the architect's model that now sat on his shelf.

Gasps filled the room. Athena knew this was quite an honor. "Yes, that sounds wonderful," she said, delighted that he liked her work so much.

"Wonderful indeedy!" Sparks flew as Zeus rubbed his hands together. Everyone ducked for cover. "My temple just happens to have twelve empty spots for paintings, and the artists will have to start tomorrow to be done in time for the grand unveiling ceremonies!"

Huh? thought Athena. *Wait a minute. Was it possible that Zeus had put Heracles and her through all this just so he'd have some ideas for his artists in time to*

actually *whisper*! Straightening, Zeus boomed out to Heracles, "Bring your tapestries by my office tomorrow morning, boy! I'll need to borrow them for a few days."

"Sure thing, Principal Zeus!" Heracles clasped the tapestries to his chest as if he regarded them almost as highly as his club.

As they all left, Athena wound up walking beside him. Aphrodite, Artemis, and Persephone were a little farther behind, carefully picking their way through Zeus's office and marveling over the weird stuff they came across.

"I'm glad you'll be staying," Athena told Heracles.

He kinked an eyebrow at her. "Really?" he said in a flirty tone.

"Yes," Athena said. And before she could chicken out, she slipped her hand into his.

Heracles almost dropped the tapestries. He glanced down at his feet. "We aren't wearing winged sandals."

"I know," said Athena. If ever there was a time and a place for just acting on her feelings, surely this was it.

He grasped her hand tightly and whistled off-key as they continued down the hall. And when he smiled down at her, she wisely smiled back.